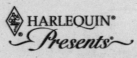

HARLEQUIN®
Presents

What can you expect in Harlequin Presents books?

Passionate relationships

Revenge and redemption

D1011956

Emotional intensity

Seduction

Escapist, glamorous settings from around the world

New stories every month

The most handsome and successful heroes

Scores of internationally bestselling writers

Find all this in our March books—on sale now!

Don't be late!

He's suave and sophisticated.

He's undeniably charming.

And, above all, he treats her like a lady….

But beneath the tux, there's a primal passionate
lover, who's determined to make her his!

Wined, dined and swept away by a
British billionaire!

Lee Wilkinson

THE CARLOTTA DIAMOND

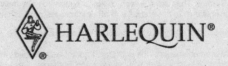

HARLEQUIN®

TORONTO • NEW YORK • LONDON
AMSTERDAM • PARIS • SYDNEY • HAMBURG
STOCKHOLM • ATHENS • TOKYO • MILAN • MADRID
PRAGUE • WARSAW • BUDAPEST • AUCKLAND

ISBN-13: 978-0-373-12618-7
ISBN-10:   0-373-12618-2

THE CARLOTTA DIAMOND

First North American Publication 2007.

Copyright © 2005 by Lee Wilkinson.

This edition published by arrangement with Harlequin Books S.A.

® and TM are trademarks of the publisher. Trademarks indicated with
® are registered in the United States Patent and Trademark Office, the
Canadian Trade Marks Office and in other countries.

www.eHarlequin.com

Printed in U.S.A.

All about the author...
Lee Wilkinson

LEE WILKINSON attended an all-girls school, where her teachers, often finding her daydreaming, declared that she "lived inside her own head," and that is still largely true today. Until her marriage, she had a variety of jobs, ranging from PA to a departmental manager, to modeling swimsuits and underwear.

As an only child and avid reader from an early age, she began writing when she, her husband and their two children moved to Derbyshire. She started with short stories and magazine serials before going on to write romances for Harlequin Mills & Boon.

A lover of animals—after losing Kelly, her adored German shepherd—she has a rescue dog named Thorn, who looks like a pit bull and acts like a big softy, apart from when the postman calls. Then he has to be restrained, otherwise he goes berserk and shreds the mail.

Traveling has always been one of Lee's main pleasures. After crossing Australia and America in a motor home, and traveling round the world on two separate occasions, she still, periodically, suffers from itchy feet.

She enjoys walking and cooking, log fires and red wine, music and the theater, and still much prefers books to television—both reading and writing them.

CHAPTER ONE

Farringdon Hall, Old Leasham

RUDY had just arrived at the door of the sickroom and raised his free hand to knock, when he heard his brother-in-law's low, well-modulated voice, and paused to listen.

'So what exactly is it you want me to do?' Simon was asking.

'I want you to try and trace Maria Bell-Farringdon, my sister,' Sir Nigel's voice answered.

Sounding startled, Simon said, 'But surely your sister's dead? Didn't she die very young?'

'That was Mara, Maria's twin sister. They were born in 1929—I was three at the time—so Maria will be in her mid-seventies by now, if she's still alive…'

His curiosity aroused, Rudy stayed where he was, his ear pressed to the door panel.

'The last time I saw her was November 1946. Though she was barely seventeen at the time, she was pregnant and unmarried. Despite a great deal of parental pressure, she refused to name the father, and after a terrible row, during which she was accused of bringing disgrace on the family, she just walked out and vanished without a trace. Our parents washed their hands of her, and her name was never again mentioned. It was just as if she had never existed. But in March 1947 she wrote secretly to me, saying she'd given birth to a baby girl. The letter had a London postmark—she was living in Whitechapel—but no address. I raised as much money as I could—I was still at college then—and waited, hoping she would contact me again, but she didn't, and that was the last time I heard from her. After my parents died I made a couple of attempts to find her, but without success. I should have kept trying, but somehow I let it slide. I suppose I thought I was immortal and had plenty of time... The doctor doesn't agree, however. His verdict is that I've three months to live at the most, so it's suddenly become urgent that I find either Maria or her offspring.'

'Do you want to tell me why?' Simon asked.

'Of course, my boy,' Sir Nigel assured his grandson. 'It's only right that you should know.

'If you'd like to open my safe, you know the combination, and take out the leather jewel case that's in there...'

There was a faint sound of movement, then Sir Nigel continued, '*This* is why. It's come to be known as the Carlotta Stone. Some time in the early fifteen-hundreds it was given to Carlotta Bell-Farringdon by an Italian nobleman who was madly in love with her. For generations it's been passed down to the eldest of the female line on her eighteenth birthday. Mara—who had a heart defect—died as a child, so the diamond should rightfully have gone to Maria, to be passed on to her daughter. Though a lot of years have gone by, it's an injustice that I would like to put right before I die, so I just hope you can find her.'

'I'll certainly do my best, but at the moment my hands are full with the American merger, and I'm due in New York tomorrow. However, if you'd like me to concentrate on finding Maria, I'll send someone else over to the States in my place,' Simon offered.

'No, no... You're needed there. The negotiations are very delicate and I don't want to see them fall down at this stage.'

'In that case, so as not to waste any time, I'll hire a private detective to start making enquiries immediately. Of course, it will have to be done with the greatest discretion,' Simon said.

'Quite right, my boy. In fact I'd like the whole thing kept under wraps. Not a word to a soul,' Sir Nigel warned.

'Not even Lucy?'

'Not even Lucy. For one thing, I'd prefer it if Rudy didn't get to know, and for another, I understand one of her friends is a so-called journalist. The last thing I want is for the story to get into the gossip columns. They always blow these things up out of all proportion, and I'd be extremely upset if there was any breath of scandal.'

It would serve the autocratic old devil right if there was, Rudy thought vindictively. He'd be only too happy to see Sir Nigel, his precious grandson, and the whole of the Bell-Farringdon family taken down a peg or two.

'In any case it would pay to tread carefully,' Simon said, 'keep the reason for the search a secret until we're certain we've got the right person.'

'You're quite right, of course. The Carlotta Stone is price-less, and I wouldn't want to risk it going to some imposter with an eye to the main chance.'

There was a silence, then Simon said thoughtfully, 'There's not a lot to go on, and it's quite possible, not to say probable, that Maria changed her name. However, mod-ern technology should make it a great deal easier...'

'Good morning, Mr Bradshaw.' The nurse's decisive voice made Rudy spin round and almost drop the books he was holding. 'Just leaving?'

Recovering himself, he said, 'No, as a matter of fact I was just about to knock.'

Made uncomfortable by that frosty blue gaze, he added, 'I thought Sir Nigel might be asleep, and if he was, I didn't want to disturb him.'

'Mr Farringdon came up to see him right after breakfast. I believe he's still there.' With that she disappeared into the adjoining room.

Cursing his luck at being caught eavesdropping, Rudy tapped at the door of the sickroom.

'Come in,' Sir Nigel called.

Trying to give the impression he'd only just that second arrived, Rudy went in breezily.

Sir Nigel, who was sitting in bed propped up by pillows, looked anything but pleased to see him, while Simon gave him a sharp glance from tawny-green eyes, and a cool nod.

Biting back his chagrin with an effort, Rudy returned his brother-in-law's nod.

With an uncomfortable feeling of coming in a poor second, he always felt threatened by Simon's undoubted good looks and masculinity, his air of power and authority.

Turning to the man in bed, he asked as genially as possible, 'How are you today, Sir Nigel?'

'As well as can be expected, thank you.'

The old devil was only just civil, Rudy thought petulantly. In spite of the fact that he had been married to Sir Nigel's granddaughter for almost three years, he was still shown none of the cordiality the baronet reserved for the other members of his family.

Nursing his grievance, Rudy went on, 'Lucy wanted to return these books you lent her, so she asked me to call in on my way up to town.'

'How is the dear girl?'

'Her progress is good since she's been home.'

Clearly making an effort, Sir Nigel asked, 'Won't you sit down?'

Never comfortable at the Hall, Rudy said, 'Thanks, but I must get on my way. As Simon will tell you, we're up to the neck in it at the bank. Apart from the normal grind there are evening meetings scheduled for the next few weeks. Then I have to face the journey home. It's at times like this I wish I'd never given up my flat.'

It was an old and familiar complaint.

Too many nights spent in town had made Lucy suspect him of having another affair, and she had put pressure on him to give up his rented flat.

Proving he had a human side, Simon said, 'I have to fly to New York tomorrow, so if you need to stay in town any night during the next two or three weeks you can have the use of my flat while I'm away.'

'That would help enormously.'

'I'll let you have the keys before I go.'

'Thanks. Well, I must be off,' Rudy said.

'Give Lucy my love,' Sir Nigel said.

'I will.'

His head full of what he'd overheard, Rudy closed the door behind him and hurried down the stairs.

Here he was, having to work for a living, he thought resentfully, while that old devil was talking about giving away a priceless diamond. Probably, if Maria was already dead, to someone he had never even met.

It just wasn't fair.

While he drove up to London, Rudy mulled it over. There must be some way he could turn the situation to his advantage…

Suppose he could trace Maria and her descendents before Simon got back from the States? That would give him a head start, and provide some interesting, and hopefully lucrative, options…

Failing that, he could kill the proverbial two birds with one stone—make some capital out of it and get a bit of his own back, by selling the story to the Press.

Oomphed up a little, it should be worth quite a few thousand. 'Aristocratic family…' 'Veil of secrecy…' 'Priceless diamond…' He could almost see the headlines now. 'Dying baronet seeking pregnant heiress who vanished from the ancestral home in 1946…'

Simon, who had glanced at him so sharply, might well suspect the source, but so long as neither he nor Sir Nigel could *prove* anything…

Rudy grinned to himself in anticipation.

But though he would like nothing better than to see the pair of them squirm, instinct told him the first option might be the better one, so he'd try that to start with.

Either way, what he had so fortuitously overheard would give him a chance to thumb his nose at the Bell-Farringdon family, none of whom had thought him good enough to marry Lucy…

Wall Street, New York

Some ten days later, Simon Farringdon received a report from his private detective which read:

> I was able to establish that shortly after she disappeared from home, Maria Bell-Farringdon changed her name to Mary Bell.
>
> Having checked the available records, I discovered that in March 1947, in the district of Whitechapel, a Mary Bell had registered the birth of a daughter, *Emily Charlotte, father unknown.*
>
> The address had been given as 42 Bold Lane.
>
> I kept searching, and discovered that in 1951 the same Mary Bell had married a man named Paul Yancey, who later adopted her daughter.
>
> Emily Yancey married a man named Bolton in 1967; however, the marriage ended in divorce some ten years later. In 1980 Emily had a daughter whose birth was registered as *father unknown.* Emily died some six months later. The baby, named Charlotte, was adopted by a Mr and Mrs Christie…

*   *   *

Bayswater, London.

'How do I look?' Unusually for her, Charlotte was nervous. The lilac chiffon dress, bought in a hurry during her half-hour lunch break, had looked reasonably sedate in the store. Now at its highest point the asymmetrically cut skirt seemed higher than she recalled, and the plunging neckline a lot lower.

Surveying the lovely, heart-shaped face framed in a cloud of silky dark hair, and the luminous grey eyes, her flatmate answered, 'So beautiful it's sickening.'

'No, seriously.'

'I'm being serious. I'd kill for cheekbones like yours and naturally curly hair, not to mention your ears. I always think nice ears are so sexy.'

'There's nothing wrong with your ears,' Charlotte said crisply.

'There's nothing right with them. They're seriously big, and the lobes are so long I look like a spaniel. Whereas your ears are small and neat, and you've hardly any lobes to speak of.'

'Which is a nuisance. It makes it awkward to wear earrings. But to get back to the point. I meant the dress; will it do?' Charlotte asked.

'Do? I can only hope the poor devil hasn't got a weak heart...'

The two girls had been flatmates since Charlotte had answered the door one evening, almost two years ago, to find a tall, rangy girl with spiky blonde hair and a thin, intelligent face standing there.

'I've just been next door visiting Macy,' the newcomer had announced. 'She mentioned that you had a two-bedroomed flat and were thinking of getting someone to share.'

'I've certainly been considering it,' Charlotte had admitted cautiously. Then, liking the look of the girl, 'Come on in... As you can see, the living-room isn't very big,' she went on, as the girl followed her into the pleasant room with its old bow-window. 'But the bedrooms aren't bad, there's a reasonable bathroom, and a good-sized kitchen.' She opened the various doors as she spoke.

'As far as I'm concerned it's next door to heaven after the crummy bedsit I've been living in for the past six months.'

Then, her blue eyes curious, the girl asked, 'Why do you want to share? In your place I'd prefer to be on my own.'

'I would prefer it,' Charlotte admitted honestly. 'But I don't have much choice.'

'I understand from Macy—by the way, we work for the same travel company—that you own the bookshop on the ground floor?'

'All I have is a lease on the premises, and, until sales pick up, finding the rent is proving to be a problem. I need some help,' Charlotte said.

'How much help?'

After a moment's thought, Charlotte named what she considered a reasonable sum.

'Well, if you think we could get along, your problem is solved. I'll pay my share of the rent up front, I promise I won't hog the bathroom or the kitchen—I'm not into cooking—and I'll keep myself to myself as much as possible.'

Coming to a swift decision, Charlotte said, 'That sounds fine by me.'

'Great! By the way, my name's Sojourner Macfadyen. But don't call me Sojourner, or I'm afraid I'll have to murder you.'

Smiling, Charlotte asked, 'What shall I call you?'

'Sojo will do fine.'

'When do you want to move in, Sojo?'

'The day after tomorrow?'

At Charlotte's nod, she had added, 'I think it'll work, but in case it doesn't…?'

'Shall we say a month's notice on either side?' Charlotte had suggested.

It had worked well, however, and the two girls had become firm friends. Even when the shop began to make a small profit and Charlotte could afford to pay an assistant, Sojo had stayed on.

On more than one occasion, she had remarked, 'When you're ready for me to move out, just say the word.'

But, knowing she would miss the other girl's company and lively sense of humour, Charlotte had been only too happy with the way things were…

'Who is your date, by the way?' Sojo pursued. Then, her voice sinking to a sibilant whisper, 'Is it still *the mystery man*?'

Endeavouring to look the picture of innocence, Charlotte said, 'I don't know what you mean.'

'I mean the one you've been so cagey about.'

'I've been nothing of the kind,' Charlotte denied.

'Oh, give me strength! For days now you've had stars in your eyes, and I'll swear your feet have scarcely touched the ground, but you've never breathed a word about him… I presume it *is* a him?'

'Of course it's a him!' Charlotte said indignantly.

'Well, come on, spill the beans. Tell all.'

'There's not much to tell.'

'Rubbish! You have the look of a woman who's on the brink of falling in love. I want to know whether to hold you back, or give you a push.'

'Do you need to do either?'

'Of course. What are friends for? So what's his name? Paul? David? Jeremy?'

Throwing in the towel, Charlotte said, 'Rudolf.'

Sojo gave a croak of laughter. 'Bit of a soppy name, Rudolf—' she pronounced it Wudolf '—unless you're a reindeer.'

'His friends call him Rudy.'

'Well, they would, wouldn't they? Anything's preferable to Wudolf. What's he like?'

'Rather special. He's—'

'You're blushing!' Sojo exclaimed. 'Dear me, you *have* got it bad.'

'Do you want to know or not?' Charlotte asked with a show of exasperation.

'I'm all ears... What an unfortunate phrase! But do go on.'

'He's slimly built and just about the same height as I am—'

'I wondered why you'd taken to wearing flat shoes. Fair or dark?'

'He has curly black hair and brown eyes.'

'Handsome?'

'Yes.'

'Sexy?'

'Very.'

'Rich?'

'He dresses well, and has what he describes as a "bachelor pad" in Mayfair.'

'Definitely not poor, then. Been to his pad?'

'No.'

'I take it he's asked you? Yes, I can see he has. What does he do?'

'I discovered, quite by accident, that he's with one of the leading merchant banks.'

Sojo whistled through her teeth. 'He's not one of their top men, by any chance?'

'I don't think so. But to say he's only twenty-six, he seems to be fairly high up the ladder.'

'So what's his surname?'

'Bradshaw. He's only been in England for about three years. He comes from the States.'

'How did you meet him?'

'He wandered into the shop one morning, a few weeks ago, just to browse. We got talking, and then he asked me out.'

'A quick worker. Been to bed with him yet?'

'Certainly not!'

'Want to?' Sojo asked knowingly.

'Yes,' Charlotte admitted.

'So why haven't you? Don't tell me he hasn't tried to persuade you.'

'I won't.'

Feeling her cheeks grow warm again, Charlotte gave the other girl a forbidding enough look to prevent her commenting.

'Well, if you both fancy each other like mad, why are you holding back?'

'It's too soon. Even if I am attracted to him, I can't jump into bed with a man I scarcely know.'

Sojo sighed. 'You're so beautifully old-fashioned. I'm not sure you live in the real world. If you're not careful you'll end up a desiccated virgin.'

'But we've only been out four or five times.'

'Is that all? I'm surprised he doesn't want to see more of you.'

'He does,' Charlotte admitted. 'But he isn't free as often as he'd like to be. In his line of work it seems social contacts are very important, and a lot of his evenings are taken up by business commitments—dining out with clients and suchlike. It was touch and go whether he could get tonight off.'

'Where are you off to? It must be somewhere special as you bought a new dress. Unless that's just for Wudolf's benefit?'

Ignoring that last crack, Charlotte said, 'He's escorting me to a supper party at St John's Wood, given by Anthony Drayton.'

'The literary agent?'

'Yes. He hosts one every year. Half of London gets invited—anybody who is anybody. His parties always have a different theme. Last year it was timed to coincide with a new moon, and all the ladies were asked to wear something silver.'

'What is it this time?'

'Candlelight.'

'Let's hope the fire brigade's been alerted,' Sojo said wryly.

'You're going out, I suppose?' Charlotte asked.

'Nope. I'll be all on my little lonesome.'

'Then why not come along with us? I'm sure Anthony won't mind.'

'It's not Anthony I'm worried about.'

'Rudy won't either.'

'That's a whopping great lie, and even if it wasn't, playing gooseberry is not my favourite role.'

'I'm surprised you're not going out with Mark. He seemed keen enough.'

'If anything, too keen. A regular Mr Touchy-Feely. I got so fed up with peeling his hands off, I showed him the door.'

Watching Charlotte collect a squashy evening bag and a silver fun-fur, she queried, 'Going by taxi?'

'No, Rudy's offered to pick me up. He should be here any minute.'

Stationing herself in the bow-window, where she could see the street in both directions, Sojo suggested casually, 'Why don't you ask him up for a nightcap when he brings you home?'

'Yes, I might. It's about time you and Rudy met.'

'So it's getting serious!'

'I'm not sure,' Charlotte admitted.

'In that case I'll give him the once-over before I make myself scarce, not forgetting to mention that I'm a heavy sleeper.'

'Don't you dare!' Charlotte exclaimed.

'Only joking, honestly. Hello! This looks like him now... Or at least a posh-looking car has just drawn up outside. A man with dark curly hair is getting out! He's gazing up at the window!' She heaved a rapturous sigh. 'Oh, Romeo, Romeo...'

Gathering up her coat and bag, Charlotte fled.

The September evening was cool and grey and slightly foggy. Street lamps cast an amber glow onto the damp pavements, and, surrounded by a halo of mist, shone like luminous ghosts.

Rudy was waiting for her on the pavement. Taking her hand, he drew her close and kissed her with a barely restrained passion.

After a moment, well aware that Sojo was almost certainly watching, Charlotte drew away.

Damn it, Rudy thought as he jumped into the car and started the engine. He was practically desperate. He *needed* to make some headway before Simon returned, and time was getting short.

But with a certain cool reserve, Charlotte was unlike any other girl he'd ever met, and so far, afraid of scaring her off, he'd forced himself to be relatively patient.

Now, however, restless and frustrated, he found the strain was beginning to tell, and he frowned as he joined the sluggish stream of evening traffic, and headed north for St John's Wood.

His experience had told him that she was on the verge of falling in love with him, and it was time to make his move. With the Mayfair flat still at his disposal he had entertained high hopes that tonight they might become lovers.

It would make a difficult situation a great deal easier and immeasurably increase his chances of keeping her—so long as he could come up with the right kind of story to gain her sympathy.

She was, he felt certain, the kind of woman who would stick by him once she had committed herself.

And he badly wanted her to.

This wasn't just the start of another affair, nor was it because she would shortly be rich, though that was a definite bonus. For the first time in his life he was mad about a woman, unable to concentrate on anything, hardly able to eat or sleep for thinking about her, and her cool reception of his kiss had shaken him badly.

Still, there was the whole evening ahead. Unless he'd lost his touch he'd be able to get her in the right mood before it ended. With a mouth like hers, and that underlying hint of sensuousness, she couldn't really be cold...

As they drew into the drive of their host's big house, Rudy's heart sank to see the parking apron was crowded with prestigious cars.

It sank even further when the handsome front door was opened by a liveried manservant, and it became abundantly clear that the party, which was well under way, was a glittering affair.

Beyond the chandelier-hung hall, a large candlelit room was packed with people, and well-dressed celebrities appeared to be ten-a-penny.

When Charlotte had first, hesitantly, mentioned the party, it had sounded innocuous enough. Expecting the whole thing to be obscure, quiet, dull and literary, he had promised to do his best to be free. But this affair was much bigger and a great deal less *private* than he'd bargained for.

He'd made a bad mistake in coming here, and the sooner he could get away, the better. If anyone recognised him and told Simon…

As their coats were whisked away, their handsome, silver-haired host appeared to greet them—Rudy with civility, Charlotte with enthusiasm.

'My dear, you look stunning. I'm so pleased you could come. The last time I invited you to one of these dos you cried off, you naughty girl.'

'I couldn't find an escort.'

'Now, *that* I don't believe. But should it ever happen in the future, come anyway, and I promise I'll never leave your side,' Anthony winked at her.

'Your wife might have something to say about that,' Charlotte teased.

Sighing, Anthony said, 'There are times I wish I'd stayed a bachelor gay.'

'Now, *that* I don't believe.'

He grinned. *'Touché.'*

'You must know that in the literary world yours and Renee's marriage is held up as a shining example of how good it can be.'

'It doesn't come much better,' he admitted. 'I think every man should have a wife, don't you agree?' He glanced at Charlotte's companion as if expecting some male support.

When Rudy said nothing, Anthony turned his attention back to Charlotte. 'What do you think of the theme?'

'Love it. Candles create such a wonderfully intimate atmosphere.'

'A romantic at heart! I always suspected it, in spite of that cool businesswoman air you cultivate. Now there are lots of people here you'll know, so do you want to just circulate? Or would you like me to introduce you to a couple of our new authors?'

'Just circulate, I think,' Charlotte said.

He kissed her hand. 'In that case, help yourselves to some champagne and go mingle.'

As they obeyed, and were greeted by people Charlotte knew, she introduced her handsome escort with a feeling of pride. But though Rudy smiled and acknowledged each new acquaintance politely, it soon became obvious that he was ill at ease and hating every minute of it.

She was wondering why, as most of the conversation, far from being confined to books, was general and lively, when a sudden stir indicated the arrival of the Press.

'Hell!' Rudy muttered. It was a possibility he should have foreseen, but hadn't.

'What's wrong?' she breathed, seeing the hint of panic in his brown eyes.

'Blasted photographers.'

'I can't imagine they'll be long. It's just a necessary spot of publicity.'

Turning his head, he whispered in her ear, 'Mind if I vanish for a time? If my picture should happen to get into the papers the powers that be will discover I'm not where I'm supposed to be, and that could mean big trouble.'

Feeling guilty that he'd neglected his job to come with her, she whispered back, 'Go by all means.'

He excused himself, and, putting his empty glass on the nearest table, disappeared into the crowd.

As though his exit had sparked it off, the little group they had been standing with began to break up. Some, hoping for their share of publicity, gravitated towards the photographers. Others drifted towards the adjoining room, where a buffet supper had been set out, and a piano was being played softly.

Deciding to wait where she was until Rudy came back, Charlotte accepted another glass of champagne and, setting her back against the wall, sipped it idly while she indulged in a spot of people-watching.

She was smiling, amused by the antics of the ones still trying to get their picture in the papers, when a *frisson* of awareness told her that she herself was being watched.

Standing in the shadows, Simon Farringdon thought that she was the loveliest thing he'd ever seen. No wonder Rudy appeared to be completely besotted.

Even his host, whom he knew to be happily married, clearly wasn't unaffected. Greeting him warmly, Anthony had said, 'Great to see you. I thought you were still in New York.'

'Just got back.'

'Well, I'm delighted you could drop in. Help yourself to some champagne, and if you're still looking for a perfect woman I'll introduce you to Charlotte Christie. As well as being really nice, she's a true beauty, with character. Unfortunately she already has a somewhat surly escort.'

'I think in that case I'll skip it,' Simon had refused lightly. 'You won't want any unseemly brawls at your party.'

'Charlotte is certainly the kind of woman men would fight over,' Anthony had said.

And he hadn't been far wrong, Simon realised now. That mouth and those wonderful eyes, upward-tilted at the outer corners, the prominent cheekbones and slightly hollowed cheeks, gave her the kind of haunting, poignant beauty that affected the spirit and senses and made willing slaves of men.

Or at least *some* men.

Though he could already feel a strong pull of sexual attraction, he had no intention of being one of them.

When Lucy—terrified that this time Rudy was engaged in something far more serious than his previous flings and might leave her—had begged for Simon's help, his first thought had been to find the girl and pay her off.

It had come as a nasty shock to discover that Rudy's latest amour and Maria's granddaughter were one and the same.

Then all the pieces had clicked into place. The morning Rudy had called at the Hall he must have overheard enough to arouse his curiosity and set him off on the trail of Maria or her descendants.

He'd clearly lost no time, and now he had not only a beautiful lover—if lovers they were—but also one who would soon be worth a small fortune.

Poor Lucy.

Except that Rudy wasn't going to get away with it, Simon vowed, no matter what it took, he would put an end to the affair.

The Press were departing now, and in the milling crowd Charlotte could see no one looking in her direction. But still the sensation persisted, like a cold breath of disquiet, raising the fine hairs on the back of her neck, making her shiver.

Then, turning her head a little, she saw a man standing in deep shadow beyond the range of the flickering candles. He was watching her intently.

Just for an instant their eyes met.

She recoiled from the shock as though from a blow, so unnerved that if she hadn't been in a room full of people, she would have turned on her heel and run...

'Sorry I've been so long.' Rudy materialised by her side. 'I thought those blasted photographers would never go.' Then, catching sight of her expression, 'If you're upset about it I can only—'

'I'm not.'

'You *look* upset.'

'Not with you, honestly. It's just that a strange man was staring at me.'

He laughed. 'With looks like yours you ought to be used to men staring at you.'

'This was different,' Charlotte insisted.

'So where is your strange man?'

'Over there.' She stopped abruptly; the shadowy corner where the man had been standing was empty. 'He's gone,' she said stupidly.

'So there's nothing to worry about. He was no doubt thinking of coming over to chat you up, and when I appeared he changed his mind.'

If only she could believe that. But she couldn't. Though she'd met the stranger's glance for only a split-second, she knew there had been nothing light or flirtatious in the look. It had been as cold and piercing, as lethal, as a stiletto.

She shivered.

Seeing that involuntary movement, Rudy said in surprise, 'You really *have* let it bother you.'

Then, deciding to seize his chance, he urged, 'Look, we don't *have* to stay for supper. You're obviously not enjoying the evening, so suppose we get out of here and go back to my place?'

As she began to shake her head, he added, 'If you're hungry, we can always stop for a bite to eat on the way.'

'I've got a better idea,' she said. 'When you take me home, instead of just dropping me off, come in and I'll cook you some supper.'

He hesitated. Ending up at *her* flat wasn't quite what he'd had in mind, but it was still a big step forward. It was the first time she had invited him back, so presumably the flatmate she'd mentioned would be out and they would be alone.

'That sounds great,' he said with a smile.

As far as he was concerned, one bed was as good as another, and in some ways it would be safer. If they went back to the Mayfair flat there was always a chance that they might leave some trace of their presence, and it wouldn't do for Simon to find out. Though his brother-in-law never swore or raised his voice, he was formidable when angry.

Rudy sighed. While he was still beholden to Simon, he couldn't afford to rock the boat. But once he had Charlotte and her money in the palm of his hand, it would be a different story.

CHAPTER TWO

'LEAVING SO soon?' Anthony asked in surprise, when they went to say their thanks and goodbyes.

'I'm afraid Charlotte has a migraine coming on,' Rudy said mendaciously.

'Oh?' Turning to Charlotte, Anthony said, 'I didn't know you suffered from migraine. Nasty things. Do you get them often?'

Charlotte, who had never had a migraine in her life, answered, 'No, I don't.'

'Just as well. I've always found that—'

'We'd better be off,' Rudy broke in quickly. 'The sooner she's in bed, the happier I'll be.'

'I'm sure.' Anthony's voice was dry.

In silence they retrieved their coats and were shown out. As they walked towards the car, Charlotte asked vexedly, 'Why on earth did you tell Anthony I had a migraine?'

'I had to tell him something.' Rudy sounded sulky.

'Anthony's no fool. He knew perfectly well we were lying to him.'

'And that bothers you?'

'Yes, it does rather. So far we've had a good professional relationship—'

'Which obviously means a great deal more to you than *our* relationship,' Rudy groused.

'No, of course it doesn't. But goodness knows what he's thinking.'

'Does it matter a toss what he's thinking?' Rudy demanded angrily.

27

Charlotte bit her lip. All in all it had been a far from pleasant evening, and now they were quarrelling.

'No, I suppose not,' she said, slipping her arm through his.

But it *did* matter. And they both knew it.

The knowledge cast an additional blight on the evening, and during the journey back to Bayswater the tension was palpable. Charlotte could think of nothing to say, and Rudy drove in a moody silence, a scowl marring his handsome features.

His bad mood was by no means improved when they reached the flat and Sojo, who had apparently seen the car draw up, opened the door.

Finding that Charlotte and he wouldn't be alone after all came as a nasty shock. Though so far everything had gone wrong, he'd been cherishing high hopes that a kiss-and-make-up situation might be just what was needed to get her into bed.

Now, seething with rage and disappointment, he realised that all his hopes were undoubtedly dashed and, after battling to come tonight, he'd be no further forward in his plans for Charlotte.

It was only too obvious from his expression how he felt, and Charlotte found herself wishing that she had never invited him back.

At that point, if he'd announced his intention of going, she would have made no attempt to stop him. But as he continued to stand there staring resentfully at Sojo, she took a deep breath and introduced them.

'Hi! Pleased to meet you,' the blonde said with casual cheerfulness. 'Come on in.'

'Rudy's staying to eat with us,' Charlotte explained as they went inside.

Looking horrified, the other girl protested, 'I know it's

my turn to get supper, but I do hope you're not expecting me to cook?'

'No. I've already volunteered.'

Taking Rudy's coat, Sojo hung it on the rack and, ushering him towards the couch, told him, 'Which is just as well if you want to stay on friendly terms with your stomach.'

Plonking herself down beside him, she went on, 'Cooking is definitely not my strong point. When it's my turn to get supper we usually have sandwiches or a take-away. It's Charlotte provides all the culinary delights. So what have we to look forward to, chef?'

'Will a quick paella do?'

'Wonderful!' Sojo said. 'I'll be happy to set the table, and wash up afterwards.' Then, turning to Rudy, 'I understand you come from the States. Which part?'

'Though my family now live in New York, I was born on the West Coast,' Rudy replied.

Sojo sighed. 'One of my dreams has always been to drive down Route 66.'

'I once did it with a group of teenaged friends in a battered old Chevy...'

Furious with Charlotte for spoiling the evening, and with some idea of getting his own back, he set himself out to be charming to Sojo.

She responded by hanging on to his every word and fluttering her eyelashes at him, while Charlotte went through to the bedroom to exchange her dress for a belted chenille housecoat, before starting supper.

While the paella finished cooking, Sojo set the table and opened a bottle of Frascati, though she herself only drank fruit juice.

When they sat down to eat and she reached to pour the wine, Charlotte shook her head. 'Thanks, but I've had more than enough champagne. Rudy?'

'I think I will have a glass.' He spoke to Sojo rather than Charlotte.

While the uncomfortable meal progressed and the conversation gradually faltered and died, his face growing ever more moody, he emptied the bottle.

Looking on, Sojo said nothing.

As soon as their plates were empty, concerned because he was driving, Charlotte made some strong coffee and re-filled his cup several times.

When he rose to go, she asked carefully, 'Are you sure it's wise to drive? If you want to leave the car where it is, we could always ring for a taxi.'

'No need, I'll be fine,' he answered ungraciously. Shrugging into his coat, he added, 'It isn't as if I'm para-lytic.'

Feeling miserable and apprehensive, she accompanied him downstairs and opened the street door.

Seeing he was about to leave her without a word, she put a hand on his sleeve. 'I'm afraid the evening hasn't been much of a success.'

'No, it hasn't.'

'I'm sorry.' Unwilling to let him go without making some effort at reconciliation, she put her arms around his neck and touched her lips to his.

He pulled her close and, his passion fuelled by anger and frustration, began to kiss her with a fierceness that was punitive.

Shaken, she took a moment or two to realise that, framed in the lighted doorway, they were clearly visible to anyone passing. Disliking the idea of being on show, she made a determined attempt to free herself.

Angered afresh by what he saw as her rejection, he turned away abruptly.

'Rudy,' she addressed his retreating back, 'when will I see you again?'

'I'll be in touch,' he promised shortly.

With a heavy heart she closed the door and returned to the flat to find Sojo standing by the window.

Glancing over her shoulder, the blonde said drily, '*Wasn't* he delighted to see me?'

Shaking her head, Charlotte said, 'It wasn't just that. Earlier we'd had a bit of a tiff.'

'I wondered why he was venting his anger on you. What did you have a bit of a tiff about?'

Charlotte explained.

'It doesn't seem much to put him in such a foul mood. Unless he's the kind of man who hates to be wrong-footed.'

Then curiously Sojo enquired, 'Why did you want to leave the party so early? Or is that a rude question?'

'Rudy wasn't enjoying it, and I was upset. You see, when I was on my own for a while I noticed a man standing watching me.'

Seeing the look on Charlotte's face, the other said sharply, 'What happened? Did he insult you in some way?'

'No. He just kept staring.'

Relaxing, Sojo opined, 'He was probably hoping to get off with you.'

'That's more or less what Rudy said when he got back, but it wasn't that kind of look at all.'

'What was this strange man like? Tall? Short? Young? Old?'

'I don't really know,' Charlotte said helplessly. 'It was all over in a split-second. He was standing in deep shadow, and all I noticed were his eyes. A moment later, when I tried to point him out to Rudy, he'd vanished.' She shivered.

Sojo frowned. 'It isn't like you to get all upset over nothing.'

'It wasn't nothing. There was so much animosity in his look. I felt...unnerved... I didn't want to stumble across him again, and when Rudy suggested that we left I couldn't wait to go. I just wish he hadn't lied to Anthony.'

'As that seems to have started it all, I bet he's been wishing the same.'

'I'm sorry he was in such a bad mood, especially when I wanted you to like him.'

'I take it you didn't warn him I'd be home?' Sojo said.

'No.'

'Well, at least seeing him in a not so good light gave me a more rounded view than if he'd been on his best behaviour.'

'So what *did* you think of him?' Charlotte asked.

'I thought he was every bit as handsome as you said. Very Byronic. I fancied him something rotten.'

'I'm glad you liked him in spite of everything.'

'I didn't say that,' Sojo pointed out.

'But you said you fancied him.'

'I *lusted* after him. But lust has very little to do with liking.'

'Then you didn't like him?' Charlotte was dismayed.

'No. And before you get any ideas, it wasn't just because of his mood. In some ways that was understandable. I dare say he was hoping to kiss and make up, big time, and finding me waiting must have been a nasty blow. Disappointment's a sharp thorn,' Sojo added reflectively, 'and if he'd *tried* to make the best of things I would have given him full marks. But he was petty and vindictive, which is an unpleasant combination. If you just wanted to jump into bed with him, have yourself some fun and then walk away, I'd say go for it. But I know that isn't your scene, and I'd hate to think of you getting emotionally involved with a man like that.'

Her voice a little uncertain, Charlotte said, 'My, you have got it in for him.'

'I don't want to see you get hurt, and if you let yourself fall for him you will be.'

'How can you be so sure after just one meeting?' Charlotte asked.

'In case you haven't noticed, he has a petulant mouth and a weak chin. Oh, and while I'm being completely frank, I don't think he's to be trusted.'

'What makes you say that?'

'Experience.'

Seeing Charlotte's downcast expression, she added, 'You know what they say, *Good judgement comes from experience. Experience comes from bad judgement.* I'm not just being rotten... And I'm not trying to put you off him because I fancy him myself.'

'No, I know you're not.'

'I just feel there's something not quite right about him. But now I've had my say, forget it. You're not a child. What you do with your life is up to you. If you're already emotionally involved, I'll just have to hope I'm wrong. By the way, does he have a minder?' Sojo asked.

'A minder?' Charlotte echoed.

'You know, someone who keeps tabs on him to make sure he's OK.'

'No. What on earth gave you that idea?'

'When you set off for the party, a silver car followed you.'

'Why shouldn't it? It's a public road.' Charlotte shrugged.

'Later there was some kind of disturbance outside—a drunk, I think. I was still at the window when you drew up. A silver car followed you back.'

'There must be hundreds of silver cars in London.'

'It was the same one,' Sojo insisted.

'A coincidence, surely.'

'It parked a little way up the street and when he drove

away just now, it followed him again. Too much of a co-incidence, wouldn't you say?'

'It certainly seems odd. Next time I see Rudy, I'll mention it to him,' Charlotte said thoughtfully.

'When are you seeing him again?'

'I'm not sure. He said he'd be in touch.'

'Presumably when he gets over his pique,' Sojo said drily.

The following morning when the girls were just finishing their toast and coffee, the phone shrilled. Charlotte answered.

Sounding rushed and flustered, Rudy said, 'I've only got a second. A short while ago my boss rang to say I'm needed in New York. Which is a blasted nuisance, but there's no way I can get out of it.'

'When will you be going?' Charlotte asked.

'I'm off to the airport now. The company car will be picking me up any second.'

'How long will you be away?'

'At the moment I've no idea. Not too long, I hope. I'll be in touch as soon as I get back...'

Before she could even say goodbye, he was gone.

'That was short and sweet,' Sojo commented. 'Wudolf, I take it?'

'Yes.' Charlotte frowned. 'Apparently his firm is sending him to New York.'

'For good?' She sounded hopeful.

'No.'

'When will he be going?'

'He should be on his way to the airport now.'

'Funny he didn't mention it last night when we were talking about the States,' Sojo commented.

'His boss only told him this morning.'

'Now, that's what you might call short notice. How long will he be gone for?'

'He doesn't know.'

As Sojo's eyebrows shot up, she added, 'But he said he'd be in touch as soon as he gets back.'

'I wasn't aware all the communication links between the US and the UK had been scrapped.'

'When he's working he's probably too busy to think of anything else,' Charlotte excused.

Sojo grunted. 'If you ask me, he's fed up with getting nowhere and he's giving you the brush-off in favour of fresh fields and pastures new.'

Then, seeing Charlotte's face, 'Sorry, that was uncalled-for.'

'Not at all; you may well be right.'

'If it's going to cause you serious pain, I'd sooner be wrong.'

'Not too serious,' Charlotte said as lightly as possible. 'And if he's the sort to do that, then I'm better off without him.'

'That's what I like to hear! Lord, is that the time? If I'm late for work I'll be hearing things I *don't* want to hear. By the way, I won't be in for a meal tonight. It's Mandy's birthday, and a gang of us are going to paint the town. Want to join us?' Sojo asked.

'No, thanks.'

'Sure?'

'Quite sure. The last time I joined your gang it took me a week to recover.'

'What's the point of painting the town if you don't do it in style? And as it happens I've some holiday due to me that I have to take before the new year, so when tomorrow's over I don't need to go into work until next Thursday. Four mornings of sleeping in late. Four whole days with nothing to do but laze about. Sheer bliss.'

'You know perfectly well that by Tuesday you'll be bored to tears,' Charlotte pointed out with a smile.

Sojo grinned. 'How well you know me. So maybe I'll do

a bit of sketching. The old man who lives across the road has an interesting face. See ya!'

When the other girl had hurried off, Charlotte cleared away and washed the breakfast dishes. Then, dressed in a grey skirt and top, her hair in a neat chignon, went down the back stairs to the shop.

One side was taken up by rows of shelves. On the other, between book-lined walls, there were several comfortable armchairs interspersed with low tables.

A hotplate, cups and all the necessary paraphernalia for 'help yourself' coffee were on a nearby trolley.

Providing free coffee for customers had proved a great success. Browsers, who in the past would have walked out empty-handed, now frequently stayed to drink and read, and ended up buying.

Having unlocked the shop door, she put two glass jugs of coffee on to heat, and brought fresh milk from the small fridge in her storeroom-cum-office.

The old-fashioned bell jangled discordantly and an elderly man came in and headed for New Fiction. He was followed by two women, then a moment later by a young man she guessed was a student, who made for the second-hand section.

Fridays were quite often busy, and this looked like being busier than usual. As well as needing to update the computer files and chase up some special orders, there was still yesterday's delivery of new stock to be unpacked.

Margaret, who normally dealt with such tasks, was on holiday until the following day. A retired librarian, she had proved to be a godsend, and during the last week Charlotte had missed her help.

But it would be as well to keep busy, she told herself firmly. It would leave little time for too much thinking or repining.

*   *   *

Simon Farringdon paused outside the double-fronted shop that in gold lettering above the old bow-windows proudly bore the legend:

Charlotte Christie
New Books Old Books Rare Books and First Editions

Then with the air of someone going into battle, he pushed open the door and went inside.

Charlotte was in the storeroom when the doorbell jangled again. It was followed by the tinkle of the small brass bell that sat on the counter alongside a card reading, *Please Ring For Attention.*

She hurried out to find a tall, broad-shouldered man, with thick fair hair and a lean, aristocratic face, waiting.

He was somewhere in his late twenties or early thirties, she guessed, and extremely well dressed, with a quiet air of authority and self-confidence.

Level brows, several shades darker than his hair, high cheekbones, a strong, bony nose and a mouth that was at once austere and sensual made him one of the most fascinating men she had ever seen.

Becoming aware that she was doing what Sojo would have described as gawping at him, she pulled herself together and said with a smile, 'Good morning.'

The thickly lashed eyes that met hers were greeny-gold, like the surface of the sea with the sun on it.

Eyes you could drown in.

'Miss Christie?'

'Yes.'

'Good morning. My name's Simon Farringdon...' His voice was clear and low-pitched. An attractive voice.

'How can I help you, Mr Farringdon?' she asked pleasantly.

'I got in touch with you recently, on my grandfather's behalf, concerning a set of rather obscure books, *Par le Fer et la Flamme*, by the eighteenth-century writer Claude Bayeaux…'

'Of course… I'm so sorry, I'm afraid for a moment your name didn't register. Your grandfather must be Sir Nigel Bell-Farringdon?'

'That's right.'

'I'm pleased to say I've managed to find the volumes he wants.'

'Excellent! He'll be delighted.'

His white smile sent little shivers chasing up and down her spine.

'I'm hoping they'll be delivered later this morning. But if not, they'll certainly—'

'Excuse me,' a shrill, impatient voice broke in, 'but do you have a copy of *The Old Fig Tree*…?'

Dragging her gaze away from Simon Farringdon, Charlotte found there were several people waiting.

'It's by Rachel Radford,' the woman went on.

'If you just give me a minute, I'll check,' Charlotte assured her politely.

'I haven't got a lot of time.'

Simon Farringdon said quickly, 'As you're obviously up to the neck, and I'd like a chance to discuss the books with you, perhaps you'll have lunch with me?'

'I'm afraid my assistant is on holiday until tomorrow, so I won't be able to leave the shop,' Charlotte said regretfully.

'In that case, dinner tonight. If you give me your address I'll pick you up at seven-thirty.'

It wasn't until later that she found herself wondering at his calm certainty, how sure of himself he'd been.

Now, feeling a strange surge of excitement, she found herself saying, 'I live above the shop.'

'Seven-thirty, then.' He sketched a brief salute and was gone.

The woman looked pointedly at her watch.

'I'm sorry,' Charlotte apologised. 'I'll only be a moment or two.'

For the remainder of the day she was on the go constantly, managing only a snatched sandwich and a cup of coffee at noon.

Though there was no time for actually *thinking*, Simon Farringdon stayed in her consciousness like a burr clung to clothing.

It was almost a quarter to seven before the last customer departed and she was able to lock the door. Dog-tired, both mentally and physically, she climbed the stairs back to the flat to shower and change.

Normally, feeling as she did, she would have looked forward to a quiet night by the fire, but now she felt a fresh surge of excitement and anticipation at the thought of dining with Simon Farringdon.

Disconcerted by his effect on her, she told herself crossly not to be a fool. This wasn't a date, it was simply a business dinner.

But even that stern reminder failed to dim her sense of expectancy.

Wondering where he was likely to take her, she was trying to decide between a midnight-blue dinner dress and a simple black sheath, when, catching sight of the dress she had worn the previous evening, she realised with a little shock of surprise that she hadn't given Rudy a single thought.

Simon Farringdon's attractive face and those extraordinary green-gold eyes had driven everything else from her mind.

How could she have believed herself on the verge of falling in love with one man, and within twenty-four hours be obsessed by thoughts of another? Especially a man she had met only briefly.

It wasn't like her at all.

Finally deciding on the black sheath, she dressed and—unusually for her, having very little personal vanity—made up her face with care.

Then, hoping for a businesslike look, she re-coiled her cloud of dark hair into a chignon. A style that, had she known it, emphasised her long neck and pure bone structure and gave her an appealing air of fragility in spite of her height.

She had just slipped into her coat and picked up her bag when the doorbell rang. Feeling ridiculously nervous, like a girl on her first date, she took a quick glance out of the window. A sleek silver car was standing by the kerb.

As she hurried down the stairs to open the door it occurred to her that, having magnified his image in her mind into something special, seeing him again she could well be disappointed.

She wasn't. If anything the impact was stronger.

Dressed in a well-cut dinner jacket, his tanned face smoothly shaven, the light from the street lamp gilding his corn-coloured hair, he would have been almost any woman's dream escort.

Taking her hand, he said, 'You look absolutely delightful, Miss Christie.'

He seemed even taller and more charismatic than she remembered, and her voice wasn't quite steady as she said, 'Thank you, Mr Farringdon.'

'Won't you call me Simon?'

'If you'll call me Charlotte.'

'It's a deal.' He smiled at her and her heart turned over. 'By the way, I've reserved a table at Carmichaels. I hope you approve?'

Carmichaels was one of the smartest dining and dancing places in London.

With an outmoded courtesy that she found quite charming, he helped her into the car. Then, sliding in beside her, he reached over to fasten her seat belt. Just for an instant his arm brushed her breasts.

That touch, brief as it was, sent heat running through her and made every single nerve in her body leap uncontrollably.

Her cheeks grew hot and, afraid he would notice, she turned her head and stared resolutely out of the side-window while he fastened his own belt.

She was still tingling when the engine purred into life and, having checked his mirror, he pulled out to join the traffic stream.

Totally thrown by his overpowering *masculinity*, and her instinctive feminine response to it, Charlotte found herself thinking in startled wonder that no other man had ever made her feel like this.

Not even Rudy.

When she was sure she could keep her voice steady, striving to sound cool and businesslike, she said, 'I'm pleased to say the books your grandfather wanted were delivered this morning.'

'That's great. How many volumes are there? Apart from noting their publication in 1756, the family archives were unclear as to the precise number.'

'There are six in the set.'

'Have you had a chance to look at them yet?'

'Only a brief glance, but they appear to be in excellent condition. Of course they're a collector's item, and rare, which is reflected in the price,' Charlotte commented.

'Apart from some historical detail I doubt if they would be of much interest to anyone but the Farringdon family or a collector,' he replied.

'I must admit I'm curious to know how they came to be written.'

'In March 1744 Claude Bayeaux, writer and poet, married Elizabeth Farringdon, and, discovering that there were strong French connections—several of the Farringdon men had taken French wives—began to research the family history. Apparently he found it absorbing, and those six volumes—which took him practically twelve years to write—trace the fortunes of the Farringdons from the 12th century up until the 18th...'

'The title *Par le Fer et la Flamme* suggests they were fairly militant,' Charlotte murmured.

'How very diplomatic,' Simon mocked, with a glinting sideways glance. 'In truth, going to war was their way of life. They changed allegiance whenever it suited them and fought for the highest bidder, tactics that made them rich and powerful, not to mention *feared*. The Farringdon women made their mark in other ways. Many of them, noted beauties with strong characters, married into other powerful families, and wielded influence rather than swords. With one notable exception. In the 15th century, Nell Farringdon is said to have killed her elderly husband, the Earl of Graydon, with his own sword, because he had betrayed one of her brothers...'

Charlotte was still listening, fascinated, as they drew up outside Carmichaels. In a privileged position overlooking Hyde Park, it was quietly discreet on the outside, openly opulent on the inside.

The latest smart society venue, it smacked of money and privilege—public school, Oxbridge, skiing in the winter, taking the family yacht to Monte Carlo in the summer.

In such a setting Charlotte could easily have felt underdressed and overwhelmed, but strangely enough she didn't. With Simon Farringdon's hand at her waist, she felt supremely confident.

When they had been greeted with deference and her coat had been whisked away, they were shown to a table on the edge of the dance floor.

Most of the other tables were occupied, and a few couples were already dancing to an old Jerome Kern tune played by a six-piece orchestra.

As soon as they were seated, and had been handed gilt-edged menus, the wine waiter appeared with a bottle of Bollinger's Recemment Degorge in an ice bucket. Having eased out the cork, he poured the sparkling wine, and waited for Farringdon's nod of approval before moving away.

Smiling at Charlotte, Simon lifted his glass in a silent toast.

She smiled back and took a sip. It was the finest champagne she had ever tasted, and she said so.

'I hoped you'd like it.' He looked straight into her long-lashed eyes, eyes of a clear dark grey with an even darker ring round the iris.

His look was so direct it was more like being touched than looked at. After a moment, her head spinning, she dragged her gaze away and tried to concentrate on the menu.

God, but she was lovely, he thought, studying that haunting heart-shaped face with its wide mouth and delicately pointed chin, the neat little ears tucked close to her well-shaped head and that long, graceful neck...

Now he knew what poets meant by swan-like.

And though she might have neither morals nor scruples, she had class. She wasn't the kind of woman he could have paid off, even if the Carlotta Stone hadn't been rightfully hers. So that left him with only one alternative. To seduce her away from Rudy.

Which would be no hardship.

Glancing up, she was shaken afresh to find that Simon was still studying her closely, a lick of flame in his eyes that made her stomach clench.

'Seen anything you fancy?' he asked smoothly, indicating the menu.

'Lots. I just can't decide.' To her annoyance, she sounded breathless.

'Do you like fish?'

'Oh, yes.'

'Then may I suggest Sole Veronique, followed perhaps by the blackcurrant cheesecake?'

'Sounds delicious,' she agreed.

His glance brought the waiter hurrying.

When their order had been given and they were alone once more, he asked, 'Is there a current boyfriend?'

Taken by surprise, she stammered, 'N-not exactly.'

He waited, his eyes on her face.

When she made no attempt to elaborate, he said, 'Tell me about yourself. What made you decide to keep a book-shop?'

'I've always liked books, so it seemed the right thing to do, especially as I had quite a lot of stock that I'd inherited from my mother.'

He raised a brow in tacit enquiry.

'She used to run a second-hand bookshop in Chelsea be-fore she remarried and went to live in Australia,' Charlotte explained. 'I'd hoped to take over her business when I left college, but the premises were due for demolition, so when I was offered a lease on the shop I have now and the ac-commodation above it, which was quite nicely furnished, I snapped it up.'

'And it's worked well?'

'Yes, very well indeed. At first I had a bit of a struggle financially, but now sales are up and I'm able to afford an assistant.'

'How long have you been in business?'

'About two and a half years.'

'Not bad going,' he said admiringly.

As the orchestra started to play a quickstep, he rose to his feet and held out his hand. 'Would you care to dance?'

The mere thought of being held in his arms made her go funny all over, and as she hesitated he added with the faintest hint of derision, 'Or perhaps you only disco?'

'I'd love to dance,' she said coolly. Rising to her feet, she put her hand in his and quivered as shock waves ran through her.

CHAPTER THREE

DRAWING her into his arms, Simon held her firmly, but not too tightly, nor too closely. Even so her pulses began to race and her knees turned to jelly.

She sent up a silent prayer of thanks that although she was shaken, and hadn't danced for some time, she had enough experience not to miss a step or stumble.

Which was just as well, as he proved to be an extremely good dancer, light on his feet and innately graceful, with a natural sense of timing and rhythm.

Though Charlotte was five feet eight inches in her stock-inged feet, the top of her head was just on a level with his mouth. Used to being as tall as her partner, if not taller, she found this heightened her newly awakened sense of femininity.

As they moved in perfect unison round the floor, she glanced up, and, seeing his quizzical expression, felt a little thrill of triumph.

Bending his head, he asked, 'Now, *where* did you learn to dance like this?'

'My father taught me. Before he died, ballroom dancing was my parents' hobby.'

'I do apologise.'

'For what?'

'For daring to breathe the word *disco*.'

'Oh, I can disco too,' she told him cheerfully.

'A woman of many parts.'

He drew her closer and they enjoyed the rest of the dance before returning to their table.

They had just regained their seats when, with perfect timing, their meal arrived. It proved to be delicious, and for the most part they ate in an appreciative silence.

It wasn't until they were at the coffee stage that Simon picked up the threads of their earlier conversation by remarking, 'You said your mother went to live in Australia?'

'Yes, she married a businessman from Sydney. I was surprised when she agreed to go all that way; she'd always hated the thought of flying.'

Thoughtfully, she added, 'To be honest, I hadn't really expected her to remarry. She and Dad were such a devoted couple. As I told you, my father died when I was eighteen.'

'Any brothers or sisters?' Simon enquired.

'No, there was just me. My parents couldn't have any children. I was adopted.'

'That's tough.'

She shook her head. 'I was one of the lucky ones. My adoptive parents were nice, decent people, and though they brought me up strictly, they loved me and gave me everything I needed.'

'What age were you when you were adopted?'

'I was just a baby.'

'So presumably you don't remember anything about your natural parents?'

'Nothing at all. I only know what Mum told me as soon as she thought I was old enough to understand, and what I picked up from the letters and documents she'd kept.'

Responding to his tacit interest, she went on, 'I know my real mother's name was Emily Charlotte, and that in 1967, when she was just twenty, she married a man named Stephen Bolton. But some ten years later it seems he left her for another woman. She was working as a secretary when she became involved in an affair with her boss, who was a married man. On discovering that she was pregnant, she appealed to him for help. Apparently he tried to persuade her to have an abortion, and when she flatly refused, he washed his hands of her. Unfortunately she'd lost both her own parents and had no one to turn to.'

'It must have been a hard time for her. So what year were you born?'

'1980. It appears to have been a difficult birth that she never fully recovered from, and six months later, weak and depressed, she caught flu and died before anyone realised how ill she was.'

'So you were Charlotte Bolton before the Christies adopted you?' Simon observed casually.

'No. After her husband left her, my mother reverted to her maiden name of Yancey.'

'An unusual name,' he commented.

'Though my grandparents lived in London, a letter written to my grandfather, Paul Yancey, suggested that he might have been born in Georgia.'

'Any idea where your grandmother originated?' he asked almost idly.

'None at all. The only thing I know about her is that her name was Mary.'

With a smile, she added, 'Unlike the Farringdons, my ancestry is a closed book, and I'm afraid it will have to stay that way.'

'Who said, *if ignorance is bliss it's folly to be wise*? The Farringdons are a pretty unconventional bunch to belong to,' Simon pointed out with a wry smile.

Then as the orchestra began to play a tango, dismissing the past, he asked, 'Shall we dance?'

This time she went into his arms without hesitation, as if she belonged there.

The rest of the evening passed, on Charlotte's part at least, in a haze of excitement and pleasure, while they talked and danced.

Though Simon drank hardly anything, he kept her glass

topped up, and when twelve o'clock came and they started for home, she was still on a high and just the slightest bit squiffy.

By that time the traffic had thinned somewhat, and they made good time back to Bayswater through the midnight streets. When they drew up outside the shop, he unfastened his seat belt and turned towards her.

Wondering if he was about to kiss her, she felt every nerve in her body tighten, and her lips parted, half in panic, half in anticipation.

When he just sat and studied her face in the mingled light from the dashboard and street lamp, feeling foolish, she rushed into speech. 'Thank you, it's been great fun. What do you want to do about the books? Would you like to take them with you, or shall I send them on?'

'That's one of the things I meant to talk to you about, but somehow the time has just flown. Perhaps you'd care to read this?'

He felt in an inner pocket, and, handing her an unsealed envelope, flicked on the interior light.

She withdrew the single sheet of thick cream notepaper, to find it covered with a laboured scrawl, which read:

Dear Miss Christie,

My grandson has informed me that you have succeeded in finding the set of books he contacted you about. I would like the chance to thank you in person, and I would be pleased if you could bring them down yourself and spend the weekend at Farringdon Hall, as my guest.

Nigel Bell-Farringdon.

Completely thrown, she stammered, 'D-does he mean this weekend?'

'Yes.'

'Oh, but I have to be in the shop tomorrow.'

'Didn't you say your assistant will be back by then? Couldn't she cope for one day?'

'Well, I suppose so, but...'

'But what?' Simon asked.

'I'd need to ask her... And it's such short notice when she's just come back from her holiday. Perhaps if I made it next weekend?'

'Next weekend might be too late,' Simon stated abruptly.

'Too late?'

'My grandfather is extremely ill. He could die at any time.'

'Oh.' She was nonplussed.

'So we're trying to comply with his every wish.'

'I quite understand, but I—'

'When he expressed a desire to meet you, I offered to write the note for him. But, though he was in great pain at the time, he insisted on writing it himself. It took a great deal of will-power on his part,' Simon added quietly.

Moved, she agreed, 'Very well, I'll certainly come if Margaret can take care of the shop.'

'He suggested sending a car for you, but I told him I would be delighted to pick you up.' Then, as if it was all settled, 'Shall we say ten o'clock?'

Apparently having achieved what he'd set out to do, he left his seat briskly and came round to open her door and help her out.

Thrusting the note into her bag, she fumbled for her key. When she finally located it, Simon took it from her and turned it in the lock.

Then, his head tilted a little to one side, he stood looking down at her, almost as if he was waiting for her to make some move.

After an awkward pause, she said in a rush, 'Thank you again for a lovely evening.'

'It was my pleasure.'

She was wondering if he was expecting to be invited up, when he touched her cheek with a single finger. 'Goodnight; sleep well.' Turning on his heel, he walked away.

That lightest of caresses made her heart beat faster and her legs were unsteady as, closing the door behind her, she made her way up the stairs.

Without putting on the light, she crossed the living-room and looked out of the window.

The street was empty. His car had gone. She felt a keen disappointment, a sense of loss, that for one idiotic moment made her want to cry.

You've had too much champagne, she told herself silently, and now you're getting maudlin.

In any case he hadn't gone forever; she would be seeing him again in the morning.

That train of thought brought its own doubts and uncertainties. What on earth had she been thinking of to let herself be railroaded into spending the weekend at Farringdon Hall?

The shop was far too busy to leave Margaret to cope on her own. So why hadn't she said so, and politely refused the invitation?

Partly because she'd been touched by Sir Nigel's note, and partly because she'd wanted very much to see Simon Farringdon again.

There! She'd admitted it.

But it was sheer stupidity to give way to such feelings. A man of his age and eligibility was almost certainly married or in a long-term relationship. And even if by some miracle he wasn't, the grandson of Sir Nigel Bell-Farringdon was way out of her league, and the sooner she accepted that, the better...

As Charlotte stood gazing abstractedly down into the street, she saw a taxi draw up and her flatmate's lanky frame climb out and cross the pavement.

There were quiet footsteps on the stairs and a moment later the door opened and Sojo crept in. On spotting the dark figure standing by the window, she gave a yelp of fright.

'It's all right,' Charlotte said quickly. 'It's only me.'

'What are you trying to do?' Sojo demanded. 'Give me heart failure?'

'Sorry if I startled you.' Charlotte was contrite.

'Why on earth are you hovering there in the dark?'

'I was looking out of the window.'

'I thought you'd be in bed.'

'I've only just got in.'

Sojo reached for the switch by the door and flooded the room with light. 'Yes, I can see you have. What happened? Did Wudolf have a change of heart and decide not to go to the States after all?'

'No, nothing like that.'

'But something's happened, I can see by your face. You look bewitched, bothered and bewildered. Let's have a hot drink, and you can tell me all about it.'

'Don't you want to go to bed?' Charlotte asked.

'Do you?'

'I doubt if I could sleep if I went,' Charlotte admitted.

'Then I suggest you get it off your chest.'

While they sat in front of the living-flame gas fire and sipped mugs of hot chocolate, Charlotte related the events of the day and evening, ending, 'When we got back, Simon gave me a note from his grandfather. Though Sir Nigel is very seriously ill, apparently he wants to meet me.'

She found the note and handed it to Sojo, who read it avidly, before exclaiming, 'What fun! Fancy being invited to the ancestral home, as well as being wined and dined by Sir Simon Farringdon.'

'He doesn't seem to use his title.'

'Well, whether he calls himself Sir or not, he sounds really something.'

'He's certainly very attractive.' Charlotte tried hard to appear underwhelmed.

Throughout her recital she had stuck to facts and left out her feelings, but Sojo wasn't fooled for an instant. 'You have the kind of dazed look that suggests you still don't know quite what's hit you. Tell me, how many times have you thought of Wudolf today? No, don't bother to answer; I can see by your face. Well, all I can say is, the lord be praised.'

Then shrewdly, 'Unless it's out of the frying-pan into the fire. What do you know about our Simon?'

'Apart from the fact that he's Sir Nigel's grandson, very little. And this proposed trip to Farringdon Hall—'

'*Proposed?* You are going, aren't you?'

'I will if Margaret can manage.'

'Of course she can manage,' Sojo blithely insisted.

'Well, if I *do* go, it's just business.'

'Business my foot!' Sojo said inelegantly. 'It's my bet that young Simon suggested the visit.'

'He's not that young.'

'So it wouldn't be cradle-snatching?'

'Of course not. He must be somewhere in the region of thirty.'

'Perfect. All you have to do is smile at him and you'll be home and dry.'

Charlotte shook her head. 'The Farringdon family are blue-blooded and wealthy; they live in a different world. I'd never fit in.'

'Stuff and nonsense. With a face and figure like yours and the voice and manners of a lady, you'd fit into an aristocratic background as if you belonged. And speaking of aristocratic backgrounds, where exactly is Farringdon Hall?'

'It's about twenty miles from London, somewhere near Old Leasham.'

'Know anything about it?' Sojo asked.

'When Simon Farringdon first got in touch with me, purely as a matter of interest I looked it up in *Britain's Heritage of Fine Historical Houses*. It's described as "A small, but delightful Elizabethan manor house, with thatched dovecotes and a charming walled garden…"'

Reaching out a hand, Charlotte took a thick volume from the bookshelf and flicked through the pages. 'Here, read it for yourself.'

The book balanced on one knee, Sojo read aloud,

'Built on the site of a much older, fortified house, and surrounded by a large estate, Farringdon Hall has been the home of the Bell-Farringdon family for almost five hundred years. During her heyday, Queen Elizabeth I is rumoured to have made many private visits there. The interior of the house is noted for its splendid fireplaces, superb oak panelling and fine plasterwork, but the highlight is undoubtedly the Great Chamber with its magnificent barrel ceiling. There are three oak staircases rising from the panelled hall. The two rear ones lead up to the old nursery suite and the attics, which have remained unaltered since the house was built, while the main staircase leads to the family rooms, one of which is said to be haunted…

'Fantastic!' Sojo, who was into ghosts, gave an excited wriggle. 'I must say I'm starting to envy you. A ghost *and* Simon Farringdon in the same house! What more could you possibly ask?'

When Charlotte finally got to bed, though she hadn't expected to, she slept almost as soon as her head touched the pillow.

In spite of having had such a late night, she awoke at her usual time and, pulling on her robe, went through to the kitchen to make a pot of coffee and a rack of toast, before phoning Margaret.

Almost before she had finished explaining, Margaret said, 'Of course I'll take over for you.'

'It's bound to be busy,' Charlotte pointed out. 'Are you sure you can manage?'

'My niece will be more than willing to lend a hand. She's always liked books. The part-time job she had during the summer is finished, and as an out-of-work ex-student she can use a spot of pocket money.'

'That's great.'

'So you just go and enjoy yourself.'

Instead of reiterating that it was just business, Charlotte said, 'I'll certainly try.'

Appearing in the kitchen in her pyjamas, her blonde hair in wild disarray, Sojo helped herself to coffee and toast before enquiring, 'I take it that was Margaret. Can she manage?'

'She's going to get her niece to help.'

Spreading butter and marmalade with a liberal hand, Sojo observed with satisfaction, 'So you're all set. With a bit of luck you might even see the ghost.'

'I'm not terribly sure I want to,' Charlotte said.

Sojo sighed. 'You have no sense of the dramatic. The scenario goes like this… You see the ghost and, scared stiff, you scream. Simon Farringdon comes running. You fall into his arms and… Well, I'll leave the rest to you and propinquity.'

'Thanks,' Charlotte murmured drily.

'Just one thing; once you get ensconced at Farringdon Hall I hope you'll remember all my helpful advice and invite me down. Oh, and when he does get round to proposing, and a man of his class will—he'll need children to inherit everything—I'll be your bridesmaid.'

'He may already have a wife and family,' Charlotte pointed out.

'You didn't find out if he was married? What on earth were you doing with your time?'

'I could hardly ask him,' Charlotte objected.

'Though surely he can't be,' Sojo thought aloud. 'If he was, he wouldn't have been rash enough to take another woman out dancing and dining.'

'But this wasn't a *date*,' Charlotte emphasised. 'It was simply a business dinner.'

'Go away! You'll be telling me next that you're not quivering like a jelly at the mere thought of seeing him again... Now I must dash... When you get back I shall expect a blow-by-blow account of all that's happened... And don't forget, so long as he's not actually married you have my permission to go get him.'

When she had showered and dressed, trying to keep her excitement under control, Charlotte selected what she was taking for the weekend, and packed it.

Well before ten o'clock she was ready and waiting, her small case zipped up and Sir Nigel's set of books replaced in the strong cardboard carton they had been delivered in.

Aware that she mustn't let Simon Farringdon see what a devastating effect he had on her, for the past hour she had been lecturing herself on the necessity to appear cool and in control.

Afraid that anything less businesslike might give the wrong impression, she had put on a fine wool suit in aubergine, and taken her hair up into a neat coil.

She was standing in the bow-window when, punctually at ten o'clock, a dark blue car drew up outside and Simon climbed out.

Her heart beating faster, she gathered up her belongings

and forced herself to walk down the stairs and open the door without undue haste.

He was waiting on the doorstep, casually dressed in a well-tailored grey sports jacket and cords. Though she was wearing high heels, he still seemed to tower over her.

'Spot on time,' he congratulated her.

That white smile, and the way his lean cheeks creased, made her breath come faster and threatened to destroy her hard-won composure.

'You have a different car.' She said the first thing that came into her head.

'Yes. I picked my own car up from the Hall this morning. The previous one was hired when I got back from the States a few days ago.'

Taking the case and books, he stowed them in the boot before helping her into the passenger seat.

As he slid in beside her, remembering what had happened the previous evening, she panicked and fumbled for her seat belt.

Straight-faced, he asked, 'Sure you can manage?'

'Quite sure, thank you,' she assured him, and realised by the gleam of amusement in his tawny eyes that he knew perfectly well what effect he had on her, and was enjoying teasing her.

It wasn't a comfortable realisation, and now it was too late she admitted that she'd been an absolute fool to come. She had known from the beginning that he was right out of her league, yet she had still allowed her desire to see him again to overrule her common sense.

So, having made the mistake, she was stuck with it. Somehow she *had* to play it cool and refuse to let him throw her.

Though that might be easier said than done.

As they drew away from the kerb, he asked, 'No problem with the shop, I hope?'

'No. Margaret has a niece who'll be willing to lend a hand.' She was pleased that her voice sounded comparatively steady.

'Good. In that case you can stop worrying and just sit back and relax.'

But how was she to relax when she was so aware of him? When in spite of all her resolve, his sheer masculinity posed such a threat to her composure that she was still trembling inwardly?

Sensing her unease, and deciding there was no point in making her wary, he went on mundanely, 'As the weather's still beautiful, it should prove to be a nice journey, and hopefully make a pleasant start to the weekend...'

His voice held only a host's concern for his guest, and a quick glance at him told her that his manner had altered subtly, and for the moment at least he did not pose an active threat.

'Grandfather is most anxious that you should enjoy your visit.'

'I'm sure I will,' she lied. Then carefully, 'I was very sorry to hear how ill Sir Nigel is. I hope he'll soon be a lot better.'

'Unfortunately we can't hope for much in the way of improvement. His illness is terminal. All the doctors can do is keep him as comfortable as possible and relatively free from pain.'

Shocked, she said, 'It must be very difficult for him to cope with a visitor at a time like this.'

'On the contrary, just knowing you were coming has pepped him up enormously. He's always enjoyed the company of women, especially beautiful ones, and since Grandmother died last summer I think he's been lonely. Though he'd never admit it.'

'Then your parents don't live at the Hall?' Charlotte asked.

'They used to—both my sister and I were born there—but they were killed in a car crash when I was six and Lucy was just a baby. Our grandparents brought us up.'

'And you both still live there?'

'I do.' She saw his jaw tighten, before he added, 'But Lucy's married now and lives near Hanwick.'

'Still, Sir Nigel has you.' Somehow she resisted the temptation to mention a wife.

'Unfortunately I'm not always here. I've had to be in the States quite a lot on business, and even when I am in the UK I'm usually only home at weekends. I stay at my London flat during the week.'

In spite of everything her heart lifted. It didn't sound as if he had either a wife or a live-in lover.

'Since Grandfather's been seriously ill, I would have preferred to commute so I could be on hand at night in case anything happened. But he wouldn't hear of it. He hates to be regarded as an invalid. In some ways it's a pity I'm not married. It's always been Grandfather's dearest wish that I should take a wife, settle down in the ancestral home and raise a family.'

'Why haven't you?' The question was out before she could prevent it.

A shade wryly, he said, 'I've been waiting to meet a woman I wanted to be with for the rest of my life.'

He changed the subject abruptly. 'Now, shall we have some music?'

'That would be nice,' Charlotte agreed.

'What kind do you prefer?'

'I like most classical music, including some grand opera. And I'm fond of comic opera, especially Gilbert and Sullivan…'

'How delightfully old-fashioned,' he teased. 'But do go on.'

'I like some jazz, some middle-of-the-road, some pop tunes—especially the older ones.'

He nodded approvingly. 'It seems we share very similar tastes. One of which we can perhaps indulge later this evening.'

She gave him an uncertain glance, and he explained, 'As luck will have it, there's a Gilbert and Sullivan charity concert tonight at the Oulton village hall. The newly formed local Amateur Operatic Society are singing a selection of songs from *HMS Pinafore, The Mikado, The Gondoliers* et cetera, and, as a patron, I was sent a couple of tickets. I had intended to give them to Mrs Reynolds, our housekeeper, but if you're agreeable it might be fun to go.'

'I'd love to.' It would pass the evening, and there'd be no danger of being left alone with him.

He flicked open one of the car's compartments to show a collection of CDs. 'So what's it to be?'

'Gershwin?' she suggested.

A few seconds later the car was filled with the haunting strains of 'Rhapsody in Blue'.

The weekend weather had been forecast as unsettled, with a front working its way through that would bring heavy rain and gale-force winds. But at the moment, as Simon had remarked, it was a beautiful day. The blue sky was cloudless and sunshine poured down, lighting up the autumn foliage and ricocheting from the gleaming bonnet of the car.

With a little sigh, Charlotte settled back to listen to the music and enjoy the drive as much as possible.

The CD had come to an end, and after her late night she was half dozing, when Simon's voice penetrated the pleasant haze.

'This is the village of Old Leasham we're just going through. It's a sleepy little place now, but in the past it was an important staging post, as you can tell by The Post-Horn, which is an old coaching inn.'

'I gather Farringdon Hall is fairly close?' Charlotte remarked.

'The main entrance is about a mile further on, while the Hall itself lies midway between Old Leasham to the south, and Oulton to the north. This is the boundary wall just coming up.'

Beyond the last cluster of white cottages a high wall built of old lichen-covered stone came into view. With an ornate tower on the corner, it formed a right angle, running left along Farringdon Lane, a narrow tree-lined track that bordered the estate, and straight on along the main road.

When they reached the imposing entrance, Charlotte saw it was guarded by two ferocious-looking lions on plinths, one each side of the tall black and gold wrought-iron gates.

A security camera perched on top of a metal pole scanned them, and a moment later the gates slid aside. As they drove through, a uniformed man appeared from the gatehouse.

Sliding down the car window, Simon enquired, 'What is it, Jenkins?'

'May I enquire how Sir Nigel is?'

'In good spirits, still.'

'Mrs Jenkins has made some of the special crab-apple jelly Sir Nigel is so partial to. Would it be in order to send a pot up?'

'Of course. I'll take it now if you like.'

Beaming, Jenkins disappeared to return almost immediately with a small muslin-covered basket.

Putting it carefully on the back seat, Simon said, 'I'm sure Grandfather will thoroughly enjoy it. Please thank Mrs Jenkins.'

'That I will, sir.'

As they drove away, he gave them a smart salute.

For a mile or so the road wound through rolling, lightly wooded parkland, on fire with the reds and golds and copper tints of autumn. Finally the colourful drifts of fern and bracken gave way to cultivated gardens surrounded by thick yew hedges cut into fantastic shapes.

They came to the Hall itself through an archway of yew, and, though Charlotte had known more or less what to expect, the first sight of it brought a gasp of sheer pleasure.

Calling it delightful had been no exaggeration, she thought. Built of mellow stone, it was both graceful and symmetrical, with a short wing at either end and a central door.

Its mullioned windows were uniform, apart from one wide, three-tiered expanse that rose roof height, and must be, she guessed, the window of the Great Chamber.

Bringing the car to a halt on the gravel, Simon sat without speaking, watching her entranced face.

When she finally turned to him with shining eyes, he queried, 'Do I gather you like the old place?'

'It's lovely,' she answered simply.

Having helped her out and retrieved her case and the carton of books, as well as the crab-apple jelly, he said, 'It isn't all that big. Apart from the attics and the servants' quarters, there are only nine bedrooms. After you've met Grandfather and had lunch, I'll show you round.'

As they approached the heavy, black-studded oak door it opened, and a plump, elderly woman with a kind face and grey curly hair appeared to lead them into a beautifully panelled hall.

Simon made the introduction. 'Charlotte, this is Mrs Reynolds, our housekeeper… Ann, Miss Christie.'

'How do you do?' Charlotte murmured.

Returning her friendly smile, the housekeeper said, 'I'm pleased to meet you, Miss Christie. If you'll follow me, I'll show you—'

'As Cook's ill,' Simon broke in, 'if you want to get on with lunch, I'll take Miss Christie up. Which room have you given her?'

'Sir Nigel suggested the Bluebell Room.'

'Very well. What time is lunch? If possible I'd like to see Grandfather first.'

'The sooner the better.' Mrs Reynolds gave her opinion briskly. 'If necessary I'll hold the meal back. In all the years I've been at the Hall I've never known Sir Nigel to be so impatient.'

'In that case, we'd better not keep him waiting any longer than we can help... If you can put this in the pantry?' He handed her the crab-apple jelly.

Carrying Charlotte's case and the books, he escorted her up the main staircase, elaborately carved in oak, and turned right along the landing.

Opening the second door on the left, he ushered her into a cosy room simply furnished with a double bed, a wardrobe, a bow-fronted chest of drawers and a cushioned armchair.

The wallpaper was patterned with a woodland scene of bluebells and green leaves, while the carpet, pleasantly faded by time, picked up the colours.

A small black fireplace was screened by a tall pitcher of cream and pink gladioli, and the casement windows were partly open, the balmy air wafting in the scent of thyme and late roses.

Putting her case on the padded window-seat, Simon remarked, 'I'm pleased to say that some years ago a central-heating system was installed and *en suite* bathrooms were added to most of the bedrooms...'

Opening a door papered to blend in with the walls, he revealed a well-appointed bathroom. 'Perhaps you'd like a few minutes alone to freshen up?'

Feeling curiously nervous about meeting Sir Nigel, and unwilling to delay matters, she said, 'I'm ready now, if you are.'

CHAPTER FOUR

HE LED the way down a wide corridor with panelled walls and oak floorboards and tapped at the door of what was obviously the master bedroom.

It was opened at once by an elderly nurse in a neat blue uniform, who slipped out to join them in the corridor.

'I've been trying to get Sir Nigel to have a sleep,' she told them in a hushed voice. 'He's in a great deal of pain this morning, but he's refused to have his injection until he's seen you, on the grounds that it makes him muddle-headed.'

Simon nodded and asked, 'How long?'

'Ten minutes, fifteen at the outside.'

She ushered them into the dimness and disappeared through a communicating door, closing it quietly behind her.

The warm, still air of the sickroom held the country-house scent of lavender and the hospital smell of disinfectant, but over and above all was an unmistakable atmosphere of tension.

'Is that you, my boy?' a voice demanded. 'For heaven's sake open the curtains and let some light in. I told that dratted woman I couldn't sleep, but she treats me as if I were a fractious child.'

Then eagerly, 'Have you brought our guest?'

'Yes, she's here.'

Simon drew back the curtains, flooding the room with light, then a hand at Charlotte's waist urged her towards the big four-poster.

Though she knew it was silly, she found herself holding her breath, as if something momentous was about to happen.

The man lying there was propped up against a pile of pillows. His silver hair was thick and springy, and though his face was skull-like, the transparent skin stretched too tightly over the bones, it was obvious he'd been a handsome man.

He smiled at his grandson, and Charlotte saw that his teeth were still good. The top middle two had a slight gap between them, which gave him an endearingly boyish look.

Smiling back with an expression of tenderness that brought a sudden lump to her throat, Simon said, 'Grandfather, here are the books you wanted, and this is Miss Christie.'

After studying her for a moment, Sir Nigel looked up at his grandson and said simply, 'Yes.'

Then, holding out a hand that was so thin and fragile-looking she was almost afraid to take it, he added, 'It's nice to meet you, my dear. May I call you Charlotte?'

'Of course.'

Still clasping her fingers, his grip surprisingly firm, he patted the bed with his free hand. 'Do sit down. Let me look at you.'

She obeyed, sitting down with care.

Though illness might be ravaging his body, it hadn't killed his spirit, and the dark eyes that studied her so intently were fiercely alive.

'Tell me about yourself, and how you come to be running a bookshop.'

She told him what little there was to tell, adding, 'I love it, though, with opening six days a week, it's quite hard work.'

Nodding, he said, 'My grandson mentioned that you should have been working today. I hope my invitation didn't cause you too much inconvenience?'

'None at all,' she assured him. 'Margaret, my assistant, was quite willing to take over.'

'I'm pleased about that.' After a moment or two, his fingers tightening slightly, he added, 'Thank you for coming, my dear. It does an old man good to see someone so young and beautiful.'

'Believe me, it doesn't do a young man any harm either,' Simon said lightly.

The two men exchanged glances that underlined a closeness Charlotte had only previously guessed at.

Turning his attention back to his guest, Sir Nigel went on, 'I'm delighted you were able to track down Claude Bayeaux's books. I'll take a look at them when I've had the afternoon rest my nurse insists on. I'm afraid my illness means I'm in bed a lot of the time and can no longer play the part of host. But I'm sure my grandson will see that you're not bored.'

Turning to Simon, he asked, 'Do you have any plans for today?'

'Indeed we do. I thought I'd show Charlotte round the house, then take her for a drive and a meal at the Oulton Arms, before we go on to the village hall to hear a Gilbert and Sullivan concert.'

'Good old Gilbert and Sullivan! Well, my dear, I hope you enjoy it.'

'Thank you, I'm sure I will.'

When the frail, papery hand released hers, she rose to her feet. 'Now I'd better go and unpack my things before lunch.'

'I hope you'll come to see me again before you go back to London?'

'I'd love to.' She smiled at him, and, leaving the men together, headed for the door.

Pulling it to gently behind her, she heard Simon say, 'The good Mrs Jenkins has sent you a pot of crab-apple jelly.'

'Ah, splendid woman, she never forgets...'

As she retraced her steps to her room, Charlotte's mind

was on the indomitable old man and the quiet courage he'd displayed.

Recalling what Simon had told her of the family's history, she decided that perhaps all the Farringdon men were fighters in their own way. Sir Nigel might be dying, but it was on *his* terms.

Once back in her pleasant room, she set about emptying her case. Packed with her overnight things and accessories was a grey chiffon dinner dress, and a skirt and top in shades of taupe and olive that Sojo—who was fond of bright colours—referred to with open contempt as funereal.

At the last minute, in case the weather stayed fine and Simon suggested a walk, she had added a pair of oatmeal wool trousers, a mulberry-coloured sweater, a pair of flat shoes and a hip-length jacket.

Deciding that the suit she was wearing was too formal after all, she changed into the skirt and top and brushed out her long dark hair.

She was preparing to take it up again when there was a light knock, and Simon's voice queried, 'About ready for lunch?'

Opening the door, she said, 'I won't be a minute. I just need to re-pin my hair.'

'Leave it as it is.' Taking her hand, he tucked it through his arm. 'I like it that way.'

His touch sensitised her skin and sent little electric shock waves running through her. Concentrating all her attention on not giving herself away, she failed to catch his question and was forced to say, 'Sorry?'

'I asked what you thought of Grandfather.'

'I liked him and admired his courage,' she said unhesitatingly. 'Considering how ill he is, he seemed very much in control.'

'He has extremely strong views about life and death and what comes after, which serve to give him unlimited strength. Though he's the first to admit he's made some bad mistakes and suffered some grave disappointments, on the whole his life's been good, and after what he describes as "a long and interesting innings" he isn't in the least afraid to die. He's already made it clear that when he does go, he doesn't want either a dismal wake or a period of mourning. Instead he would prefer a celebration of his life, and then for things to go on as if nothing had happened.'

Certain now that he cared a great deal for his grandfather, she asked, 'Will that be possible?'

'It may not be easy, but, as it's what he wants, I'll do my best.'

Lunch proved to be an informal affair, served by a young maid and eaten in the light and airy morning-room. The simple fare, celery soup followed by a Quiche Lorraine and raspberries and cream, was delicious, and as they drank their coffee Charlotte said so.

'Mrs Reynolds will be pleased. She prepared it herself, as the cook has flu. Incidentally, I've told her we won't be in for dinner tonight, that with your agreement we're having a meal at the Oulton Arms. I think you'll find the place interesting historically, and the food, while nowhere near the cordon-bleu class, isn't bad. However, if you'd prefer to eat somewhere more upmarket...' Simon raised an eyebrow in enquiry.

'No, the Oulton Arms sounds fine.'

'In that case, when I've shown you round the house, we'll take a leisurely drive through the estate and leave by the north gates. That route takes us through the park proper, where we graze both sheep and deer, and the wooded area.'

'Are sheep the estate's main source of revenue?' Charlotte asked.

'Not any longer. A few years ago an independent survey showed the estate was seriously overstaffed, but, as a lot of the families had been with us for several generations and wanted to stay, Grandfather was reluctant to ask anyone to leave. After consulting the people involved and listening to their ideas, we decided the best option would be to diversify and create new jobs. There were large areas of woods and pine forest standing idle, so we began to fell carefully, replanting with deciduous trees as we went. At the same time we went into pig breeding and poultry farming—specialising in rare breeds of pigs and hens—and into market gardening in a big way. The market gardening was a great success and we now have several farm shops and a growing trade in organic produce. As well as providing employment, the various ventures have proved to be extremely lucrative. Now fifty per cent of the profits go to children in need, and a charity that fights drug abuse and helps to maintain a series of hostels for the homeless…'

As well as simply being attracted, she was starting to *like* him, and she was ridiculously pleased to know that both he and his grandfather cared about people.

'More coffee?' he asked.

She shook her head. 'No, thank you.'

'Ready to begin the Grand Tour?'

'I certainly am.'

'Then I suggest we start with the Great Chamber and the Long Gallery.'

Charlotte was staggered by the grandeur of the Great Chamber, and the elegance of the Long Gallery, which was lined with family portraits that ranged from the 16th to the 20th century.

'If you're interested,' Simon said, 'I'll explain who everyone is another time. But right now we'll get on and see the rest of the place.'

'The rest of the place' was everything and more than Charlotte had imagined. As well as being serenely beautiful, Farringdon Hall had an atmosphere she could only describe as one of contentment, as if generations of being loved and cared for and lived in by the same family had made it into a real home.

'I can't imagine anywhere less likely to be haunted.' She spoke the thought aloud as, the tour completed, they were returning via her room so she could pick up her coat and bag while Simon spent a few minutes with his grandfather.

'So you've heard there's a ghost?'

· Feeling a blush starting, she admitted, 'I was curious enough to look Farringdon Hall up in *Britain's Heritage of Fine Historical Houses...*'

'I see.' There was some slight nuance she couldn't catch. 'What else did it have to say?'

'That in her heyday, Elizabeth I was rumoured to have made many private visits to the Hall.'

'I don't doubt it. Sir Roger Farringdon, a notorious rake who owned the house at that time, and had been widowed quite young, was known to be one of the queen's favourites. Next time we visit the gallery I'll show you his portrait. But to get back to our ghost...'

'You mean there really is one?'

'Grandfather certainly believes there is. This is her room we're just coming to now.'

When he opened the door Charlotte was surprised to find that it was a child's room, full of the paraphernalia of childhood—dolls and a doll's house, an old-fashioned rocking-horse, a pram with a golly in it and a cot containing a large teddy.

A jumble of books and toys were still stacked on a wide shelf. The air struck chill.

'After her death it was left completely untouched,' Simon explained.

'So she was a member of the family?'

'Oh, yes. She was Grandfather's sister. Her name was Mara and she was born in 1929. When she was still a toddler it was discovered she had a serious heart defect that in those days it wasn't possible to correct. She was just turned seven when she died.'

'And Sir Nigel believes that her spirit still lingers here?' Charlotte asked with a shiver.

'Yes.'

'What do *you* believe?'

'I keep an open mind,' he said lightly.

Charlotte would have liked to know more, but the brevity of his answer seemed to preclude any further questions.

'Now, about ready for our outing?' he queried.

'I will be in a second or two when I've fetched my jacket and bag.'

'While you do that, I'll just put my head round Grandfather's door and tell him we're off.'

Outside, the air had turned appreciably colder and a rising wind was hustling ragged, charcoal-coloured clouds across a leaden sky.

As they made their way through a wide stone archway to the right of the house, Simon, who was wearing a short car coat, remarked, 'It looks like the forecast's correct and we're in for some rain.'

'If I'd been thinking straight I would have packed a mac instead of a jacket,' Charlotte said ruefully.

But excitement had precluded straight thinking.

'It won't matter if it rains while we're in the car, and I'll try to park near the entrances to both the pub and the village hall... Of course if everyone has the same idea—'

'We'll just have to run between the drops,' she finished, smiling.

He returned her smile.

Watching his excellent teeth gleam and laughter lines form at the corners of his eyes, she felt her heart begin to beat faster.

The force of his attraction was powerful, as if he were

true north and she, like a magnet's needle, couldn't resist the pull.

'As we'll be going cross-country,' he told her, when they reached the creeper-covered garage block, 'what I will do is take the vehicle Frank Moon, our estate manager, uses, rather than my own car.'

Retrieving a large bunch of keys from a locked cupboard, he added, 'A lot of the roads through the wooded areas are just rutted tracks, so if it does rain heavily, we may well need a four-wheel-drive.'

Glancing around her, Charlotte observed, 'This looks like part of an old stable block.'

'It is,' he confirmed as he helped her into the big estate car. 'There are still a couple of stalls left in the other part, but we haven't kept horses since I was in my teens.'

'Did you learn to ride as a child?'

Sliding behind the wheel, he answered, 'Yes, but when I went to university there was only Lucy left and she didn't care for horses, so Grandfather gave them to a local riding school for the blind.'

As the engine roared to life and they headed north through rolling parkland dotted with grey woolly shapes, he went on, 'From time to time I've considered getting a couple of horses so I, and possibly a guest, could ride at weekends.'

Only half listening, she watched his hands on the wheel— strong, exciting hands with long, lean fingers and neatly trimmed nails—and pictured them touching her intimately, so that her breath came faster and butterflies danced in her stomach.

Making an effort to banish such erotic thoughts and concentrate, she pulled herself together, and said, 'It sounds a wonderful idea. But wouldn't you need someone to exercise them during the week?'

'Our present chauffeur used to be a groom, and he's declared himself more than willing to take them out on a daily basis.'

Then thoughtfully he asked, 'I gather you ride?'

'Yes, I learnt when I was about eleven. Of course, it wasn't *real* riding,' she added a shade wistfully. 'I used to go to a local riding school that took small groups hacking round suburbia.'

'Tell me about it.'

'I rode a black horse named Milord. Though he stood seventeen hands, he was as gentle as a lamb. The problem was, we were always trailing behind the others.'

'Why was that?'

'His mouth was so hard he was able to do exactly as he pleased. He used to amble along at his own pace, stopping whenever he felt like it to tear chunks from people's hedges and snatch whatever he could reach from their gardens. I often spent a lot of my "lesson" apologising,' she added wryly.

Watching the corner of his long, mobile mouth lift in a smile, she found herself imagining that mouth moving against hers.

As though he knew exactly what she was thinking, he turned his head and their glances met.

In that instant, as green-gold eyes looked into grey, desire flared between them with a white-hot furnace heat.

Damn! Simon thought, returning his gaze to the road. Normally his feelings were well under control, but that unexpected and unplanned explosion of lust had taken him by surprise.

Out of the corner of his eye he could see that Charlotte's face was as red as a poppy and she was staring fixedly ahead.

It was clear that the feeling had been mutual, which in some ways was satisfying. But it had come too soon.

He had every intention of seducing her, but when the time

came to put his plans into action, he didn't want her to be on her guard. It would only make things more difficult.

Feeling as though her very bones had melted like candle wax, Charlotte gazed through the windscreen, while she wondered confusedly how so much strong feeling, so much mutual passion could be whipped up in just an instant.

And surely it *had* been mutual?

A surreptitious sideways glance confirmed that Simon's jaw was tightly clenched, and a dull flush lay along his hard cheekbones.

But though he was obviously roused, he had made no attempt to take advantage of the situation. Rather he had backed off.

She felt a rush of gratitude. If he had stopped the car and touched her, she would have been lost, and to get involved with someone like Simon Farringdon would be madness.

He might be used to casual sex and one-night stands, but she certainly wasn't. And while *he* would no doubt be able to walk away afterwards without a second thought, she knew instinctively that *she* wouldn't be able to.

The experience would at best be unforgettable, at worst, scar her. Either way she would never be the same again.

For what seemed an age, but in reality could only have been a minute or so, they drove in silence. Then, unable to bear the tension a second longer, Charlotte rushed into breathless speech.

'Just a moment ago I thought I glimpsed some buildings behind those trees...'

'That's Aston Prava...' Simon's voice sounded restricted '...it was purpose-built about ten years ago to house the estate workers. Though the hamlet *looks* in period, the houses are slap up-to-date with all mod cons, and the tenants even have their own village shop and post office. Until then the outside staff had been scattered in various small cottages throughout the estate, without mains water or electricity.'

'How did they manage?' she asked abstractedly.

'With bottled gas, and water pumped from the nearest stream or their own well.'

'I can't imagine any of them minded moving.'

'The majority were delighted.' Simon's voice sounded more normal now. 'Only Ben Kelston, our old gamekeeper, asked to stay where he was. His two-up, two-down cottage is in the woods miles from anywhere, and, as he was turned sixty at the time and doesn't drive, Grandfather tried to talk him out of it. But he said firmly that he'd been born and bred at Owl Cottage—his father had been gamekeeper before him—and he didn't want to leave. While a move might have been in Ben's best interests, it would be a real shame if Owl Cottage was allowed to stand empty. It's a picturesque timber-framed, cruck-trussed building that dates from the early fifteen-hundreds.'

'It sounds delightful.'

'It's a perfect little gem. Unfortunately it's so isolated that it's unlikely anyone else would want to live in it.'

Grasping at the conversation as she would have grasped at a lifeline had she been drowning, she asked, 'So is Ben still there?'

'He was until a few days ago, when he fell and broke his hip. Frank happened to call in as he was passing, and found him lying on the scullery floor. He's in hospital at the moment, and Frank and his wife are looking after things until he's well enough to return home.'

'Will he be all right, do you think?' Charlotte asked.

'Up to now he's looked after himself well enough, and he's kept the cottage spotlessly clean.'

'But surely he won't be able to manage the stairs?'

'A few months ago, when he had a minor accident, Frank and I brought his bed downstairs, so that won't present a problem...'

To Charlotte's great relief, by the time they reached the

electronically controlled north gates any awkwardness seemed to be forgotten, and she began to look forward to the evening ahead.

In the event, it proved to be a great success. The food at the Oulton Arms was tasty and satisfying, and they both thoroughly enjoyed the concert.

Though earlier the threatened bad weather had manifested itself only as a brisk wind and some light rain, by the time they left the village hall it was blowing a gale and pouring down.

Simon took her hand and together they sprinted for the car, arriving wet and, in Charlotte's case, breathless. A condition caused more by the touch of his hand than by the run!

Jumping in beside her, he switched on the engine and turned up the heater, before passing her a folded handkerchief. 'I'm afraid this is the best I can do in lieu of a towel.'

'Thank you.' She wiped the rain from her face and hair, and handed it back.

He followed suit in a cursory manner before dropping the sodden ball of linen onto the floor.

His fair hair was darkened by water, and fine beads of moisture still clung to his eyebrows and thick lashes. She watched a single drop trickle down his lean cheek, and shivered as she felt a sudden mad urge to brush it away.

Noticing that involuntary movement, he said, 'We'd best take the most direct route and get back as quickly as we can so you don't catch a chill.'

The wipers, even going at top speed, barely managed to keep the windscreen clear as they eased carefully through the crush of home-going cars and headed out of the village.

Once they were through the Hall gates and into the wooded area of the estate, the road became littered with torn-off twigs and small branches.

Their lights making a dazzling tunnel between the trees,

he drove with even greater care, picking his way through the fallen debris.

Charlotte had turned her head to look at a swollen brown stream rushing past, when all of a sudden they swerved and left the track, coming to a halt halfway up a shallow, mossy bank.

'It's all right,' he assured her quickly, 'there's no problem. I just had to swerve to avoid a badger.'

He turned the ignition key to restart the car.

She waited for the reassuring roar, but apart from the wind and rain there was silence.

As he tried again the headlights abruptly died, leaving them in total darkness.

'Hell!' he swore softly. 'I'm afraid we *do* have a problem after all.'

'What's wrong?' She managed to keep her voice even.

'Frank said that last week the electronics had developed an intermittent fault, but this looks more like the battery. He took the car into the local garage, and when he picked it up the head mechanic assured him the fault had been fixed. But it seems he was mistaken.'

'Can you phone for help?' she asked hopefully.

'I could if I had my mobile with me. Unfortunately, I didn't bring it.'

'Oh,' she said in a small voice.

'The last time I took it to a concert I'm afraid I forgot to switch it off, and it rang in the middle of ''Silent Worship''.'

She laughed, then asked as cheerfully as possible, 'So what do we do now? Walk?'

There was a rending, splintering sound, and a sizeable branch crashed down close to the car, making her jump.

She saw the gleam of his eyes in the darkness. 'I think not. It's a devil of a long way, and apart from the fact that neither of us are equipped for it, it wouldn't be safe to walk far in this kind of weather. Our best bet would be to shelter until morning, then reassess the situation.'

'You mean stay in the car?'

'No. As we're already wet and the heater's not working, that would be much too cold and uncomfortable. Our best bet is Owl Cottage.'

'Is it far away?'

'Not more than a hundred metres or so. It's on the other side of the stream we've been running parallel to, but the bridge is just up ahead. Once at the cottage we'd be able to light a fire and have a hot drink of some kind.'

Though the thought of having a fire and a hot drink was more than welcome, she asked practically, 'Won't it be locked up?'

'Yes, but as Frank and his wife are looking after the place there should be a key on his bunch.' Having felt through the keys, he said, 'This might be it. You wait here while I go and make sure.'

From the glove compartment he took out a big, rubber-covered torch. Adding, 'I'll be as quick as I can,' he forced open the car door, struggling to hold it against the wind. A second later it slammed behind him, and she saw the beam of his torch moving away along the track.

It was already getting uncomfortably cold, and she found herself hoping against hope that it was the right key.

As though the fates were against them it seemed to be raining harder than ever, and fierce gusts of wind were buffeting the car. Somewhere close at hand she could hear more branches crashing down, and, fearful for his safety, prayed silently, *Please God, don't let anything happen to him...*

Feeling alone and vulnerable, she waited in the darkness for what seemed an age, surrounded by the noise and violence of the storm.

A movement close by that seemed to have nothing to do with the wind made her imagination run riot, and she was absurdly relieved when she saw the beam of the torch returning.

Opening the car door, Simon said, 'Quick as you can. Thank the lord this is the leeward side.'

The torchlight lit his face from beneath, giving it strange hollows and weird angles, turning it into a Hallowe'en mask.

Clutching her bag, she stumbled out.

Throwing an oilskin around her, he gathered her into the crook of his arm, and together they began to pick their way along the track, avoiding the fallen debris as best they could.

Now that she was away from the comparative shelter of the car, rain lashed into her face and the wind beat against her like a malignant force, tearing at the oilskin, taking her breath, sapping her strength.

Hampered by high heels, she knew she would hardly have been able to battle against the storm without his help.

'Almost there; just across the bridge.'

His words were whipped away by the wind almost before she'd heard them. A second later the torch briefly illuminated an old humpbacked bridge spanning the turbulent water.

They fought their way across the bridge, and almost immediately she saw a welcome gleam of light ahead, then the dark bulk of the cottage and a low stone wall surrounding a garden.

'Here we are.' The gate was swinging wildly, and he caught and held it before propelling her through. Latching it securely, he added, 'Don't want it banging all night.'

Perhaps it was half-hysterical relief that made his comment seem funny, but she found herself giggling as he hurried her up the path.

When he opened the cottage door they were swept inside by a gale of wind and rain and leaves. Shouldering the door shut behind them, he lifted the streaming oilskin from her shoulders and hung it on a peg, where it immediately began to form a puddle of water on the black oak floorboards.

Glancing around her, Charlotte saw a white-walled, black-beamed room, simply but pleasantly furnished, with a pine table and two chairs, a chintz-covered two-seater settee, several overflowing bookcases and a wheel-backed rocking-chair.

On the far side of the room was an old-fashioned double bed with gleaming brass rails and knobs. It had a comfortable-looking mattress and a small pile of pillows. Standing alongside it was a sturdy bedside table with a candle in a brass candlestick and a box of matches.

As well as lighting the two oil lamps on the dresser, Simon had put a match to the fire, and flames were already leaping and crackling round the logs in the old black-leaded range.

It was a welcome sight.

'Come on over by the fire,' he said.

She needed no second urging. Despite the oilskin, she was soaked and shivering, her teeth chattering, so that she was forced to clench them.

Simon, who was equally saturated, his hair dark and plastered to his head, water running in rivulets down his face, must have been just as cold but, she noted with respect, he gave no visible sign of it.

Drawing the heavy folkweave curtains across the windows to shut out the storm, he instructed, 'Hurry up and take off those wet things. I don't want your death on my conscience.'

When she had discarded her bag and jacket, and put her saturated courtshoes on the hearth, unwilling to undress any further in front of him, she queried, 'Is there a bathroom by any chance?'

'Yes, but I thought I'd use that. Until I've lit the water

heater and the gas lamp, and it's had a chance to warm up, it'll be like the North Pole. You'll be better in front of the fire. Now while you finish stripping off, I'll go and dig up some towels and a couple of blankets to wrap ourselves in.'

CHAPTER FIVE

FEELING awkward and exposed, but grateful for the heat the logs were already throwing out, she stood on the pegged rug in front of the fire and began to struggle out of her clothes. She had just reached her undies when she heard him coming back, and paused.

'Are you decent,' he enquired from the doorway, 'or shall I cover my eyes?' Without waiting for an answer, he walked in.

The sight of her made him catch his breath.

She was standing in front of the hearth, her slender figure outlined by the flickering fireglow, her long dark hair hanging round her shoulders in dripping rats' tails. Made transparent by the water, the dainty bra and briefs she was wearing clung to her like a second skin, hiding nothing.

Only too aware that her nipples, already firmed by the cold, were growing even more prominent under his appreciative male gaze, Charlotte felt herself start to blush.

Handing her one of the towels he was carrying, he remarked teasingly, 'Well at least you're getting some colour back.'

Blushing even harder, she clutched the towel to her chest and waited for him to go.

Draping a second towel over the rocker, he went on conversationally, 'I'm afraid Ben has a duvet these days, which means there are no blankets, so I hope you can manage with this?'

This was a lumberjack-style shirt.

'I'm sure it'll do fine,' she said hurriedly.

'Then I'll leave you to it.'

As soon as the door had clicked shut behind him she finished taking off her clothes. Then, fastening a towel turban-fashion round her head, she dried herself and pulled on the thick flannel shirt, doing up the buttons right to the neck.

It was a reasonable fit across the shoulders, and she realised its owner must be quite a small man. Still, it came a respectable length down her thighs and would be adequate so long as she moved with care.

When she had finished drying her hair, well aware that left to its own devices it would turn into a riot of tangled curls, she fished in her bag for a comb and combed it through.

At one side of the hearth was a tall three-legged wooden stool, and she draped her wet clothes over it before taking a seat in the rocking-chair and stretching her bare feet towards the flames.

Now she had a moment to think, she found herself dreading the coming night. Being stranded in an isolated cottage alone with Simon Farringdon was the worst possible thing that could have happened.

Though no doubt Sojo wouldn't have thought so. *'I'll leave the rest to you and propinquity...'* The other girl's voice seemed to echo in her head.

Shivering, though this time not from cold, Charlotte read herself the Riot Act. It was nobody's fault that they were stranded here, and as nothing could be done about it before morning, it was no use getting panicky. All she had to do was keep her cool and everything would be all right.

Though he was a red-blooded male, and it was clear from the earlier incident in the car that he was sexually attracted to her, she was quite convinced that he wasn't the kind of man who would try to force himself on her.

But then he wouldn't need to.

She tried to refute the sobering thought, but was unable to. Better to face it and plan a strategy.

No matter how much he attracted her she wasn't the type who could make the first move, so she should be relatively safe from her own impulses.

But suppose *he* turned up the heat?

Well, if he showed any sign of it she would just have to freeze him off, keep her defences intact and give no hint that she was vulnerable…

'Hot chocolate?'

Charlotte hadn't heard him coming, and she jumped.

'Sorry if I startled you.' He was wearing a wry expression and a short navy-blue towelling robe that showed five inches of wrist, strained across his wide shoulders, gaped at the chest and was only kept decent by a belt tied tightly around his lean waist.

Seeing her eyes widen, he explained, 'Unfortunately Ben is barely five feet seven and built like a jockey, so this is the only thing I can get into.'

It looked so ludicrous that she gave a little choke of laughter.

'You might well laugh,' he said grimly.

'I'm sorry.' The apology was spoiled by another irrepressible chuckle.

His face relaxed into a grin, and a moment later his low, attractive laugh joined hers.

She was pleasantly surprised. Most of the men she knew hated to be laughed at, and certainly wouldn't have been able to laugh at themselves.

Holding out one of the mugs he was carrying, Simon suggested, 'Perhaps you'd like to take yours? If I bend over or make any sudden move, I will almost certainly offend your maidenly modesty.'

Feeling the colour rise in her cheeks, she accepted the steaming mug, and, heeding the timely warning, stared resolutely into the leaping flames.

The chocolate was good and hot and relaxing, and she

rocked gently as she sipped, while Simon drank his leaning decorously against the stone mantel.

'Warm enough?' he asked.

'Yes, thank you.'

Stifling a yawn, she glanced up at him. His hair, towelled back to its normal corn-colour, was attractively rumpled and the beginnings of a golden stubble adorned his jaw.

Fighting back a mad urge to rub her cheek against it and put her lips to the strong column of his throat, she stared fixedly at his broad chest.

As he flexed shoulders that must have been uncomfortably restricted his robe gaped even more, and, fascinated, she watched the ripple of muscles beneath the smooth, tanned skin.

Suddenly becoming aware that he was watching her watching him, she dragged her gaze away with an effort and looked back into the fire.

There was silence, apart from the sound of the wind and the rain beating against the windows, and the contented ticking of an old-fashioned carriage clock.

A log settled and broke and a small piece of burning wood fell into the hearth close to where he was standing.

As her eyes were drawn to the glowing ember, she saw that his bare feet were well-shaped with neatly clipped nails, his legs firm and straight with a light fuzz of golden hair.

Becoming aware that the robe barely reached his knees, and the front edges were parting company, she looked hastily away once more and, face burning, gulped the last of her hot chocolate.

He turned what might have been a laugh into a cough, before enquiring solicitously, 'I hope it was to your liking?'

Determinedly ignoring any possible *double entendre*, she answered, 'Yes, it was fine, thank you.'

'It proved to be a choice between that and black coffee, and I thought coffee might keep you awake.'

He collected the empty mugs, and, taking her wet clothes from the stool, added, 'Now the heater's lit, if I spread these over the airing rack in the bathroom they'll dry much faster.'

The warmth of the fire was soporific and in spite of everything she was practically asleep by the time he returned carrying clean sheets and pillowslips and a maroon and cream duvet.

Forcing open eyes that felt as if they were full of sand, she looked up blearily, smothering a yawn.

'Tired?'

'Yes,' she admitted. It had been a long, emotionally draining day.

'As soon as I've made up the bed I suggest we both get some sleep.'

For the first time the full reality of the situation struck her, and she froze.

Then after a moment, relaxing somewhat, she recalled that when Simon had described the cottage he'd said *two-up, two-down*, so presumably there were two bedrooms.

But would there be another bed?

As though reading her thoughts, he said, 'I'm afraid there's only the one bed, so unless you want to share it…?'

'I don't!' Her voice had risen in alarm.

'In that case I'll take the couch.'

Her feeling of relief was elbowed aside by guilt. 'But you said there were no blankets.'

'Don't worry, I can manage with a coat. And at least there are plenty of pillows. Ben must sleep propped up.'

Sounding quite sanguine, he added, 'The bathroom is just along the passage, the first door on the left. There should be *some* warm water by now, but I very much doubt if there's enough for a shower.'

She got to her feet and, very conscious of his gaze on her bare legs, made her way along the lamplit passage to a small

bathroom, where the white porcelain fittings, though anti-
quated, were gleaming and spotlessly clean.

A gas lamp over the sink bathed the place in yellow light
and threw out a halo of warmth, and the boiler, with its little
row of blue and gold flames, popped and gurgled cheerfully.
The only real snag was a cold draught coming under the
door.

Seeing her stockings and undies hung tidily over a slatted
airing-rack alongside Simon's silk boxer shorts gave her a
strange feeling. It was almost as if they were an old married
couple.

Soap, towels, a face-flannel, a tube of toothpaste and a
bottle of shower gel had been laid out ready on a green
painted shelf.

Bearing in mind Simon's warning, she washed at the sink
rather than risking a shower, and in the absence of a brush
used a finger to clean her teeth as best she could.

When she returned to the living-room the bed was made
up, and Simon was putting more logs on the fire.

'Finished?' he asked.

'Yes, thank you.'

'Then the bed's all yours. I'll go and wash before I turn
out the lights.'

The big bed looked more than inviting and she climbed
in with a sigh, plumped up a couple of pillows and closed
her eyes.

However, her sojourn in the bathroom had turned her feet
into blocks of ice, and, as she knew that the settee would
be much too short for him and was bound to be terribly
uncomfortable, a combination of cold feet and guilt pre-
vented her from sleeping.

But it would be madness to share the bed with him, and
she knew instinctively that he was too much of a gentleman
to let *her* take the settee...

She was still wide awake, thoughts buzzing round in her

brain like bees, when he returned wearing nothing but a towel knotted around his lean hips. He was carrying a couple of coats over his arm and a blue rubber hot-water bottle.

He turned towards the bed, and in a sudden panic she feigned slumber.

'Asleep?' he asked softly.

Though her eyes were closed, she was aware that he was standing looking down at her.

She felt the bedclothes being moved gently aside and then the warmth as the hot-water bottle was slid in beside her feet.

After a second or two she heard the brush of his bare soles on the floorboards as he walked away, and released the breath she'd been unconsciously holding.

Peeping through her lashes, she watched him douse the oil lamps, then take off the towel and stretch. With the fireglow gilding his naked limbs, he looked like Apollo, and she caught her breath audibly.

She saw his teeth gleam in a smile, before he said conversationally, 'Next time you're pretending to be asleep, remember to breathe.'

When she said nothing, he pursued, 'Why aren't you asleep? Is there some problem?'

'My feet were cold,' she said in a small voice.

'Hopefully that's been taken care of.'

'And I felt mean about you sleeping on the couch,' she added in a rush.

A moment later he was sitting on the edge of the bed looking down at her.

Her hair, a riot of dark, silky curls, was spread over the white pillow. The fireglow touched her face, casting shadows, gleaming in her eyes, hollowing her cheeks.

'That could be remedied, if it's bothering you. Though it has to be your decision.'

She swallowed hard. He was much too close, much too naked, much too male.

'W-well I—I...' She stammered to a halt, averting her eyes.

'It's quite simple,' he said patiently. 'Do you want me to share your bed or not?'

When, hot all over, she continued to hesitate, he went on, 'As you could see if you were incautious enough to look, you have a powerful effect on me, so if the answer's yes, I'm afraid I can't promise to treat you like a sister.'

Common sense spoke for her. 'Then the answer's no!'

'Very well,' he said equably, 'I'll settle for the couch and a goodnight kiss.'

Her normally soft, husky voice high and shrill, she cried, 'No! No, I don't want to kiss you.'

'Then *I'll* kiss *you*.'

He placed his hands one each side of her head, palms down, trapping her hair beneath them, and bent to touch his lips to hers.

That lightest of caresses had the same effect as a lit match dropped into a keg of gunpowder.

As, without conscious volition, her mouth opened beneath his, he began to kiss her with a fierce, burning hunger that swept her up and carried her along willy-nilly.

In the past, on the few occasions she had been seriously tempted to sleep with a man, she had thought and considered and weighed up any possible consequences, and invariably caution had won the day.

But now, caution didn't get a look-in. Conscious only of an overwhelming desire, a *need* to belong to this man, she wound her arms round his neck and returned his kiss, responding to his passion with complete abandonment.

He slid in beside her, his fingers urgent as he unbuttoned her shirt and found the soft curves of her breasts, teasing the firm nipples, making her stomach clench, sending shock waves running through her.

When his mouth took the place of his fingers, her whole body convulsed in a grinding ache of longing.

She felt the hard maleness of him against the electric sensitivity of her skin, and, her throat dry and burning, she pulled him down, opening to him, welcoming his weight.

There was an explosion of ecstasy at his first strong thrust, then their bodies bucked in unison, and behind her closed eyelids the world splintered into a million fragments of black and gold.

He groaned once, softly, just as the first joyous waves of release began to shudder through her.

Both of them were breathing as if they'd run a race as, blind and deaf, she lay beneath him, his fair head heavy on her breast.

When he finally lifted himself away and gathered her close, exhausted by the day and the emotional storm she had just lived through, she was asleep within seconds.

She surfaced slowly, luxuriously, her body sleek and satisfied, her mind drifting, no thoughts of past, present or future disturbing its tranquillity.

Gradually emerging from the dreamlike trance, she realised that last night's storm had died away and sunlight was filtering round the curtains. The fire in the old black range had settled into whitish ash, and, despite the brightness, the air was cool.

But she was glowingly warm, lying cradled in the crook of an arm, her head pillowed comfortably at the juncture between chest and shoulder.

Simon's arm... Simon's chest... She could hear his quiet, even breathing, feel the beat of his heart beneath her cheek.

A cautious peep upward showed her his face intriguingly

inverted, the firm chin covered in morning stubble, the thick, dark gold lashes fanning onto his hard cheeks.

Memories came flooding in, memories of his hands and mouth touching her breasts, his weight pinning her down, memories of hunger and need, of surrender, and undreamt-of delight.

But it had been more than mere surrender. A great deal more. She had met and matched his passion with a passion of her own.

Recalling how recklessly, how *wantonly*, she had behaved, she waited to feel both shame and regret.

She felt neither, only a sense of amazement that she had lived for so many years without knowing such ecstasy existed.

Giving herself so completely to a man she scarcely knew, a man who cared not a jot for her, had been foolish in the extreme. But it had also been a new and wonderful, life-enriching experience, and she couldn't regret it.

Perhaps in the following days she would *come* to regret it, especially when Simon treated her like any other casual one-night stand.

But possibly he wouldn't just brush her off? She knew now that he could be kind and caring, so maybe he would let her down lightly? Pretend she had been just a little bit special?

But did she want that sort of pretence?

No, of course she didn't. She had always preferred honesty, even if it hurt.

And it would hurt. She knew that without a shadow of a doubt. But it wasn't as if she had fallen in love with him, she told herself hastily. It was simply that he was the only man she had ever wanted enough to make her throw caution to the wind.

She had never got into the modern way of regarding sex as merely sex, divorced from love, or sometimes even liking, just a natural appetite that could be indulged with as little soul-searching as possible.

If she could start thinking that way...

But she couldn't, any more than she could alter the nature she had been born with. The most she could do was refuse to flay herself for what had happened, to accept with gratitude the new dimension it had given her life.

Simon had promised her nothing. She had expected nothing from him. It should be relatively easy to regard last night as a one-off and walk away.

So why did it feel like the end of the world?

Perhaps because it had come and gone so quickly. She hadn't had time to grasp that moment of delight and fulfilment, to hug it to her, to savour it.

So what did she want? she asked herself crossly. The kind of affair that would drag on for a few weeks while Simon decided how to end it?

No, she didn't want that. It would be less painful in the long run to keep her chin high and pretend she didn't care. To give thanks that, if not totally unscathed, she had enough pride left to enable her to hide it.

And if all she would have left were some fleeting memories, she was still lucky. Though there might have been no love involved, at least she had known true rapture...

Unconsciously she sighed.

'Why the sigh?' Simon asked.

Glancing up, she saw the blue gleam of his eyes between half-closed lids. He looked so virile and sexy that her heart began to race uncomfortably.

Afraid he would feel it, she hastily eased herself free and, pulling the shirt together over her bare breasts, sat up.

'Not regretting it, I hope?' he pursued, pushing back the pillows and following suit.

Unwilling to let him know just how much it had meant

to her, she answered as coolly as possible, 'Why should I be?'

'I thought in the cold light of morning you might be having second thoughts.'

'If I were, it would be too late.'

'Are you?'

Looking anywhere but at him, she answered, 'No.'

'I'm rather pleased about that. I must admit I haven't been quite so impetuous since the days of my youth. Nor as careless... But I presume you are protected?' he added.

The casual question shook her rigid.

'P-protected?' she stammered.

'As in contraception?'

She could scarcely believe that she had given no thought to such an important issue. Yet, swept away by passion, she hadn't.

And now it might be too late.

Looking at her half-averted face, he added blandly, 'I've always been led to believe that modern women didn't take any chances.'

They probably didn't, she thought miserably, but she could hardly be described as a modern woman in that sense.

'So you're not?' he pressed.

'No,' she admitted in a small voice.

There was a pause, as though he was considering what she'd told him, then he said, 'Oh, well, at least we don't need to worry too much about it.'

Ruffled by his insouciance, she said stiffly, '*You* may not need to.'

'Don't you like children?' Simon asked.

'Of course I do, but—'

'Then there's no real problem,' he stated.

'I'm glad you think so.'

'We can get married—'

'*What?*'

'We can get married,' he repeated patiently.

'*Married!*'

'As there's a possibility you may be pregnant...'

'It's *only* a possibility.'

'I'd sooner we got married at once rather than waiting to be certain.'

'B-but we've only just met,' she stammered. 'We don't really know each other.'

'Both those things can soon be remedied. Do you have any other quibbles?'

'We come from totally different backgrounds,' she protested.

'Does that matter?'

'It might well.'

'I don't happen to think so. Once we're married—'

'I can't marry you,' she gasped.

'Why not?'

'Because I can't,' she insisted raggedly.

A razor-sharp edge to his voice, he asked, 'Are you in love with someone else?'

'No.'

'Sure about that?'

'Quite sure. If I'd been in love with someone else, last night would never have happened.'

He nodded as if satisfied.

'And, as I was as much to blame as you, there's no need to...' She hesitated and stopped, biting her bottom lip.

'Go all Victorian and propose?' he suggested.

'Exactly.'

Tongue-in-cheek, he said, 'Perhaps I feel that it's my duty as, at the very least, I've compromised you.'

'I wish you wouldn't joke about it.'

'Very well, I'll be serious. Hand on my heart, I'd like you to marry me.'

When she began to shake her head, his voice quizzical, he asked, 'Do I take it you can't stand the sight of me?'

'No, it's not that at all.'

'But you really don't want to be my wife?' he pressed.

She *did* want to be his wife. Shaken by the knowledge, which came clear and sharp and certain, she hesitated.

His eyes on her expressive face, he persisted, 'So what's the problem?'

Pulling herself together, she informed him, 'I couldn't marry a man who doesn't love me, who only suggested marriage because I might be pregnant.'

'But I didn't only suggest marriage because you might be pregnant. If you *had* been protected I would still have asked you to marry me.'

'You must have an over-developed sense of chivalry,' she said, her voice tart.

He raised a level brow. 'How do you work that out?'

'I take it it's because I'm a guest in your house. Presumably you don't propose to all the women you go to bed with?'

'Neither do I rush them into it.'

'As I *allowed* myself to be rushed into it, the responsibility's mine. You don't *have* to marry me,' Charlotte snapped.

'I happen to want to,' he said quietly.

'Why?'

Reaching out a hand, he took her chin and turned her face towards his. 'Would you believe it if I told you that when we met for the first time my heart stood still?'

Hurt and angered by his mockery, she said tightly, 'No, I wouldn't.'

'Pity, as it happens to be the truth.'

When, hardly able to believe her ears, she simply stared at him, he went on softly, 'I thought you were the most exquisite creature I'd ever set eyes on, and I wanted you more than I've ever wanted any other woman. Happy now?'

Suddenly she was. Ecstatically happy. 'Yes.'

'Then you'll marry me?'

'What will your grandfather say?'

'Don't worry, he'll be pleased. He took an instant liking to you.'

'I'm glad… I like him.'

'Good. But you still haven't answered my question. Will you marry me?'

She should have said she needed a clear head, time to think. Instead, under his spell, she found herself agreeing, 'Yes, I'll marry you.'

His little smile was that of a conqueror as he tilted her face up to his and kissed her.

The stubble of his beard rasped her lips and, her stomach clenching, she opened her mouth to his searching tongue.

While he deepened the kiss, forcing her head back against the pillows, his hands found the rounded curves of her breasts and the pink nipples firmed under his touch.

With a stifled gasp she ran her fingers into his thick blond hair, holding him to her, while desire rose inside her. It flowed from the centre of her being like red-hot lava, swamping everything but her need for him.

Slipping the shirt from her shoulders, he tossed it aside and eased her onto her back, kissing her closed eyelids, her cheekbones, her throat, while one hand slid down over her ribcage and stomach to the silky skin of her inner thighs.

She was shivering, but it had nothing to do with the cool air of the room, as she abandoned herself to his experienced fingers. When his mouth took the place of his fingers she had to bite her lip to stop herself crying out.

His lovemaking was infinitely skilled and gentle, coaxing the maximum sensation from her body while he kept her just on the brink.

Finally, unable to stand any more, she begged huskily, 'Please, oh, please…' and felt his weight with gratitude.

This time, showing a steely control over his own body and hers, he moved with maddening slowness. Drawing shuddering thrills from her, he withdrew to the very tip before pressing back again, creating a slow spiralling need that built into a white-hot molten core of tension.

Only when her body instinctively began to urge his did he move faster, driving deeper, until the tension exploded like a volcano. She cried out at the intense pleasure, and heard his low, answering groan.

When their heart-rate and breathing returned to normal he lifted himself away, and, gathering her up, brushed her damp, tangled hair away from her cheeks and kissed her.

Totally at peace and engulfed by a kind of languid sweetness, she fell asleep in his arms, her face against his throat.

When Charlotte awoke for the second time she was alone in the bed. Logs flamed and crackled in the grate and a welcome smell of coffee was drifting in from the scullery.

She was about to get out and pull on the shirt before fetching her clothes, when the door opened and Simon came in carrying a large wooden tray. He was fully dressed, his blond hair, still a little damp from the shower, parted on the left and tidily combed. 'Hungry?' he asked.

'Starving.'

'The best I can manage is black coffee followed by tinned sausages and baked beans. Not very exciting, I'm sorry to say, but as we've expended so much energy,' he added wickedly, 'I thought we'd better go for it.'

Trying hard not to blush, she said composedly, 'It smells wonderful.'

'As it's still none too warm out here, I suggest you have yours in bed.'

With a feeling of being cherished and cared for, she pushed herself upright and leaned back against the pillows.

Balancing the tray dexterously on one hand, he removed the candlestick and matches from the bedside table before setting it down.

She noticed that the stubble had gone from his jaw, to be replaced by a slight rawness and a drying trickle of blood. Feeling a sudden rush of tenderness, she said, 'You've cut yourself.'

'It's just a nick.' Wryly, he added, 'I'm out of practice with the kind of cutthroat razor Ben has. The only time I've used one of those was at college, and then I did it for a bet.'

'I'm surprised you bothered shaving.' She spoke the thought aloud.

'I wouldn't have done, but bristles play havoc with a delicate skin like yours—the bits I can see are still pink from last time—and I was overcome by a strong desire to kiss you all over.'

Before she could protest he drew back the duvet and, taking her hips, pulled her flat on her back. Then, growling softly, he nuzzled his face against her breasts, alternately nibbling and sucking.

While she laughed and squirmed helplessly, he worked his way down her ribcage to her slender waist. His mouth was hovering over her navel when she gasped, 'Stop...'

'I've scarcely started. I haven't even got to the really interesting bits.'

'Please stop.'

'You mean you don't like it?'

'I mean I'm hungry, and the beans and sausages will be getting cold.'

He straightened with a sigh and helped her sit up. 'What a very practical woman. I can see that in future I'm going to have to feed you before I indulge my lascivious cravings.'

Reaching for the shirt, he put it carefully around her shoulders. 'Coffee first?'

'Please.'

When their mugs were empty, he spread a clean tea towel over the duvet and put a heaped plate and a knife and fork in front of her. 'Tuck in.'

Then, sitting down companionably on the edge of the bed, he reached for his own plate and began to eat with a healthy appetite.

Watching him, Charlotte saw that, without looking anything but entirely masculine, he ate with a kind of neat precision.

Unlike some big men, all his movements were easy and graceful, and whatever he was doing he seemed to have complete control over his own body. The thought brought vivid memories of his earlier lovemaking, and made her breath come faster and her pulses race.

Leashing his own needs, he had been ardent, tender, skilful and wonderfully generous. She had never, in her wildest fantasies, imagined having such a lover.

She wanted to pinch herself to make sure that all that had happened since they'd come to Owl Cottage hadn't been just a dream.

For instance, had she really agreed to marry a man she had known for barely two days?

Incredibly, she had.

What on earth had made her do it?

She was head over heels in love, it was as simple as that. Somewhere she had read that you first fell in love with your eyes, then your emotions, then your mind. But she hadn't done it in stages, and she hadn't called it love.

Instead she had labelled this bolt from the blue physical attraction, only now realising it was love. A fierce, all-consuming love that had lit a torch and sent her up in flames...

CHAPTER SIX

'I TAKE it that, like me, you'd prefer a traditional church wedding to the register office?' Simon's voice broke into her thoughts.

'Yes, I would,' she agreed unhesitatingly.

'Good.' Putting their empty plates on the tray, he went on, 'It shouldn't take long to get everything organised. We'll need a special licence. But my godfather, as well as being an old friend of the family, happens to be an archbishop, which ought to facilitate matters. If I talk to him as soon as we get back, we should be able to get married in a few days' time.'

'A few days!' She was staggered. 'Oh, but I—'

'Grandfather doesn't have much longer, and I'd like him to live to see us married.'

'But there's the shop and—'

'Couldn't you ask your assistant—Margaret, did you say her name was—to take care of things for the moment?'

'I suppose so, but—'

'Then surely there's no problem? With regard to your flat you can just leave everything where it is until the wedding's over. Then, when you've moved your personal possessions, give your landlord notice and return the keys.'

'I don't think I'll need to do that. I'm sure Sojo will want to stay on,' she said.

'Sojo?'

'Sojo Macfadyen. My flatmate.'

Looking momentarily startled, he said, 'I didn't know you had a flatmate.'

'Oh, yes.'

'Male or female?'

'Female, of course.'

He grinned briefly. 'It's hard to tell with a name like Sojo.'

'Her name's Sojourner. Though she's liable to get violent if anyone calls her that.'

'How long has she been with you?'

'Almost two years.'

'What does she do?'

'She works for a travel company.'

'I see. Presumably you get along well?'

'Very well.'

'In that case, despite the short notice, perhaps she'll be your bridesmaid?' he suggested.

Recalling Sojo's words, Charlotte was about to say, *I'm sure she will*, when, bearing in mind the traditions accompanying weddings, she suggested, 'Shouldn't we ask your sister first?'

Brusquely, he said, 'Earlier this year Lucy was badly injured in a car crash. Part of her spine was crushed. Since then she's been bedridden and in considerable pain.'

Charlotte was shocked. 'I—I'm so sorry. How dreadful for you all.' Even as she spoke she was aware of how inadequate the words were.

As he saw her stricken face, his own face softened. 'It's been a trying time, particularly for Grandfather, who's always been very fond of her. He was extremely upset when the hospital warned us she might never walk again. However, Lucy's got plenty of courage, and she's a fighter. Now, after a couple of operations, she's back home and starting to make some positive progress. But to return to the question of a bridesmaid...'

'I'm sure Sojo will be thrilled to bits,' Charlotte assured him. 'As luck will have it, she'll have no problem getting time off work. When I get back to the flat I'll—'

'When were you thinking of going back?' he questioned sharply.

'Later today.'

'Not a chance,' he told her decidedly. 'I'm not letting you out of my sight until we're well and truly married.'

She felt a little thrill of excitement at this show of male possessiveness.

Still, common sense insisted that she should make a stand. Shaking her head, she said, 'I'll need to go back to get some clothes, and I must—'

'I've a better idea. As Miss Macfadyen has some time off work, when we get home we'll ring her up and invite her to stay with us. If you ask her to bring whatever clothes you need to tide you over, I'll send a car for her.'

The thought of inviting Sojo to Farringdon Hall was a welcome one, but there were other considerations. 'I have to talk to Margaret about the shop...'

He leaned forward to brush his lips down the side of her neck, making her shiver with delight. 'My heart's darling, couldn't you do that by phone?'

Seduced by the caress and the endearment, she admitted, 'I suppose I could.'

'That's my girl,' he said jubilantly, and planted a series of soft baby kisses along her jawline, before his mouth covered hers.

Gladly she abandoned herself to his kiss. Simon loved her. He didn't want to be parted from her for even a short time. If she had harboured any faint doubts as to his feelings, that fact alone should have been reassuring.

Having kissed her into a state of mindless bliss, he queried, 'Then everything's settled?'

She nodded.

'And you're happy?'

'Yes.' The sober answer reflected hardly anything of the joy that filled her and made her cup of happiness overflow.

Touching her cheek with a single finger, he said, 'Though I'm very tempted to stay and make love to you all morning, I'd better fetch my coat and get moving. Otherwise Grandfather will be wondering what's happened to us.'

'Is there any chance of getting the car started?' she asked when he returned almost immediately, shrugging into his coat.

'A faint one, possibly, but if I have no joy I'll start walking back.'

'If you wait until I'm dressed I'll come with you.'

He shook his head. 'It's a long way, and, though the weather looks to be reasonable this morning. it's bound to be bad underfoot.'

Remembering the previous night, and how difficult even a comparatively short distance had seemed in high heels, she gave in gracefully.

'While I'm gone, you can get a shower of sorts, and there are plenty of books.'

'I'll find something to do.' She looked at the tray and the rumpled bed.

Following her glance, he said, 'Don't worry about the dishes or the bed; I'll get one of the servants to come in and set the place to rights.'

He tossed another couple of logs on the fire, and a moment later the door closed behind him.

Struggling against the sense of loss his departure caused, she went along to the bathroom and, discarding the shirt, stepped into the bath, pulled the plastic curtain into place and turned on the shower unit.

The water was a comfortable temperature and the shower gel fresh and tangy, but instead of enjoying it she found herself thinking of Simon, wishing he had kissed her again before he'd left.

Perhaps he didn't really love her?

Her father had always kissed her mother before he went

out, even if he was only going to the local shop to buy a paper.

But she was just being silly, she scolded herself. Simon did love her. He'd said so.

All at once, in spite of the hot water, she went cold inside. He *hadn't* actually said he loved her. He had said his heart stood still, that she was exquisite, that he wanted her, but he had never mentioned the word love.

Though why would he be rushing her into marriage if he didn't love her? If it was only because of the risk of her being pregnant, it would have done no harm to wait and see, before he proposed.

Perhaps, when the chance arose, she would ask him exactly how he felt about her.

No, she would do nothing of the kind. The last thing she wanted was to become one of those insecure women who needed so much reassurance that they became pathetic, a burden to the man in their life.

After all, he hadn't asked if *she* loved *him*. So either he took it for granted, or he didn't care.

Neither was ideal, she thought as she towelled herself dry. But though she didn't want her feelings taken for granted, it had to be better than him simply not caring.

After the steamy heat of the shower the air struck chill, and, shivering a little, she reluctantly donned yesterday's undies, skirt and top and, her jacket over her arm, returned to the warmth of the fire.

She had combed the tangles out of her hair and was just knotting it loosely in the nape of her neck, when the door opened and Simon walked in.

Her spirits rising with a bound, she queried hopefully, 'How did you get on?'

'Started first time. I've left it just across the bridge with the engine running, so if you're about ready to go...?'

'All ready.' She pulled on her jacket, slid her feet into

shoes that felt a little stiff, picked up her bag and followed him outside.

It was a fine, bright morning with not a breath of wind. Sun glinted through the trees, turning a million droplets of water into diamonds and making the saturated ground steam slightly.

When he'd locked the door behind them, they made their way out of the small garden and over the old humpbacked bridge.

A noisy brown torrent was surging through the single arch, carrying branches and loose boulders that battered at the stone foundations. The force seemed to make the whole structure shake, and she was glad to reach the other side.

As Simon helped her into the car she glanced back at Owl Cottage. So much had happened there, it would always be special to her. Though if it hadn't been for the storm, the cottage wouldn't have come into the equation, and events would almost certainly have moved at a much slower pace.

But would she have wanted them to?

Before she could answer the question, following the direction of her gaze, Simon asked, 'No regrets?'

After a moment she replied steadily, 'No regrets,' and knew it was the truth.

The road through the woods was littered with storm debris and several times he had to stop the car and get out to move the bigger branches. On one occasion they were forced to leave the track altogether to find a way around a fallen tree. Once they had left the woods, however, and were into smoothly rolling parkland, they made much better time.

When they reached Farringdon Hall, Mrs Reynolds came hurrying to meet them. 'I'm glad you're here,' she said to Simon. 'Sir Nigel's been anxious since he asked for you and discovered you weren't back.'

'Thanks, Ann. Perhaps you'll let him know we're home safely and we'll be in to see him as soon as we've changed.'

A little while later when Charlotte emerged from her room dressed in fresh undies, her oatmeal trousers and mulberry-coloured sweater, Simon was waiting.

After an appreciative glance at her slim trimness, he queried, 'All set? Then we'll go and tell Grandfather the good news, shall we?'

She went reluctantly. Though Simon seemed to think his grandfather would be pleased, she seriously doubted it. Why *should* Sir Nigel welcome a working-class girl into his aristocratic family?

And the whole thing had happened far too quickly. He would probably think that in so short a time she couldn't possibly have come to love his grandson. He might even think that she was just after his money...

Glancing at her face as they made their way along the corridor to the old man's room, Simon asked, 'Feeling nervous?'

'Scared stiff,' she admitted.

'You've no need to be,' he reassured her.

'But suppose he doesn't accept me?'

'He will,' Simon said with certainty. 'He took you to his heart the moment he saw you.'

As they reached the sickroom door it was opened by the nurse, who sighed with relief. 'Thank the good lord you're back. Sir Nigel's been on edge since breakfast time waiting for you—'

'Simon, my boy,' her patient's voice cut across the discreet whisper, 'is everything all right?'

'Everything's fine.'

'Not too long, now,' the nurse cautioned, and slipped quietly away.

'We had some trouble with the car,' Simon explained,

'and because of the weather conditions we decided to stay the night at Owl Cottage.'

'Very sensible,' Sir Nigel approved.

Taking Charlotte's hand, Simon drew her to the bed. 'We have some good news, haven't we, darling?'

Looking even more gaunt and fragile, the old man was sitting propped up by pillows. His dark eyes moving from face to face, he waited.

'We're going to be married.'

Any worries Charlotte might have entertained about Sir Nigel's reception of the news were instantly set at rest. His approval was evident.

Eyes alight with joy, he said, 'Following the family tradition, eh? I can't tell you how delighted I am…Charlotte, my dear…' He held out both hands, long, thin, almost transparent hands, blotched with liver spots.

She took them gently in her strong young hands, and bent to kiss his cheek. His parchment-like skin smelled faintly of eau-de-Cologne.

Shaking hands with his grandson, he queried with undisguised eagerness, 'How soon?'

'As soon as possible,' Simon assured him. 'We would both prefer a church wedding, so I'm going to give Matthew a ring and see about an Archbishop's Licence. Hopefully, we can arrange things for Wednesday or Thursday.'

'You'll be married at St Peter's?'

'I'd like to, though I haven't yet had time to discuss this with my bride-to-be.'

Turning to Charlotte, he went on, 'Our family have been tying the knot at the village church for generations. Grandfather was married there, so were my parents.'

'That sounds lovely,' she agreed.

Obviously relieved, the old man asked, 'What about bridesmaids and a best man?'

'Charlotte is going to ask her friend and flatmate, Miss

Macfadyen, to be her bridesmaid, and, as neither of us have
got a brother to act as best man, I thought I might ask—'

Sir Nigel looked up, his jaw tight. 'Not—'

'No, no...' Simon said quickly. 'I was thinking of
Matthew's son, James.'

'Good choice,' Sir Nigel approved.

'If he can get the time off work, of course.'

'What about Miss Macfadyen? Presumably she works?'

'Yes, but as luck will have it, she has some holiday due,
so I've suggested that we invite her down for a few days,'
Simon said.

'An excellent idea!'

'Now all we need is someone to give the bride away. It's
a great pity you're not well enough.'

'Who says I'm not? I'll be only too happy to give
Charlotte away if she has no objection, and doesn't mind a
wheelchair at her wedding.'

'I'd be delighted,' she told Sir Nigel truthfully. 'So long
as it won't be too tiring for you.'

'My dear, this news has given me a new lease of life, so
I may as well use it to do something that will ensure me an
enormous amount of pleasure.'

'In that case it's settled,' Simon said.

Sir Nigel looked as pleased as Punch. 'You're having a
honeymoon, of course?'

'Eventually.' Simon's manner was deliberately casual.
'But we're in no hurry.'

'Every new bride and groom should have a honeymoon.
It's part of the tradition.'

'In the circumstances—' Simon began.

'I don't want you to stay at home because of me,' Sir
Nigel broke in. 'Couldn't you have a short honeymoon now
and a longer one when I've gone?'

'If that's what you want.'

'It is,' the old man said firmly.

'Then we'll fly to Paris or Rome for two or three nights. But obviously, before I can book anything, I'll need to get the wedding arrangements in place. So if I go and phone Matthew now...'

Taking Charlotte's hand, the old man asked, 'Would you be kind enough to keep me company for a little while? I'd like to talk to you.'

A warning note in his voice, Simon queried, 'Are you sure that's wise at the moment?'

The two men exchanged glances.

'Maybe I am being impatient,' Sir Nigel agreed with a sigh.

'You're looking very tired,' Simon pointed out gently, 'and there's no point in knocking yourself up before the wedding.'

'Yes, I'm sure you're right. God willing, there'll be time for Charlotte and I to get to know one another after the pair of you are married. Now, give my warmest regards to Matthew, and do invite Miss Macfadyen to stay at the Hall...'

The nurse, who had just returned, said with frosty disapproval, 'I really must insist, Sir Nigel, that you get some rest now.'

He raised his eyes to heaven, before agreeing with suspicious meekness. 'Very well, Nurse.'

Releasing Charlotte's hand, he told her, 'You've made me very happy, my dear.'

Then to Simon, 'Perhaps you'll come up later and let me know how things are going?'

'I'll be up after lunch,' Simon promised.

As they descended the stairs, reaction setting in, Charlotte said shakily, 'He was so *pleased*. I thought at the very least he would be upset by the suddenness, the *speed*... After all, we've only known each other two days.'

'Falling in love at first sight seems to run in the Farringdon family,' Simon remarked.

So he did love her...

Her heart singing, she asked, 'Is that what your grandfather meant when he talked about following the family tradition?'

'Yes. My great-grandparents were married within a few weeks of getting to know each other—though Sophia, my great-grandmother, was Italian and spoke very little English—and Grandfather asked Grandmother to marry him less than six hours after meeting her.'

'What about your parents?'

'My father proposed to my mother three days after they met. He had to propose twice more before she accepted him, but the circumstances were different. She was a young widow and still in mourning for her husband, who had been killed by a terrorist bomb. Though my grandparents' and great-grandparents' marriages were long ones, and my parents' marriage tragically short, they were all very happy.'

It seemed a good omen, and, her gladness overflowing, Charlotte slipped her hand into his.

Just for an instant, as if his mind was elsewhere, he failed to respond, then his fingers closed around hers and gave them a squeeze.

When they reached the sunny living-room, he suggested, 'If you give me the phone number of your flat, I'll have a quick word with Miss Macfadyen. Then you can fill her in on all the details while I talk to Matthew.'

She told him the number, and he tapped it in.

On the second ring the receiver was lifted and Sojo's voice said laconically, 'Hello?'

'Miss Macfadyen, this is Simon Farringdon...'

'Simon Farringdon...' she echoed. Then sharply, 'Is there something wrong? Where's Charlotte?'

'There's nothing wrong; in fact everything's fine, and

Charlotte is here with me now. She tells me that you're on holiday, so I'm ringing to invite you down to Farringdon Hall for a few days.'

'Is this some kind of joke?' Sojo demanded.

With a rueful glance at his companion, Simon denied, 'Not at all. Charlotte and I would very much like your company.'

After a pause, Sojo said cautiously, 'Well, if you really mean it, I suppose I could get a train down. When do you want me to come?'

'If you have no plans for this afternoon?'

'No.'

'Then I'll send a car for you. Say three o'clock... Now Charlotte has something to ask you, so I'll leave her to explain.'

He handed over the receiver and went into the library, which also served as his office-cum-study.

Doing her utmost to curb her excitement, Charlotte said, 'Sojo?'

'What's going on? Why do you want me to come down?'

'Nothing's *going on*, but quite a lot's happened.'

'Like what?'

'Like Simon and I are going to be married.'

There was a stunned silence on the other end of the line, then Sojo laughed. 'You're kidding, of course.'

'I've never been more serious.'

'Honestly?' Her voice squeaked a little.

'Honestly.'

'That ghost must have been quite something.'

'It had less to do with the ghost than being stranded overnight.'

'Stranded overnight! Hang on a minute... OK, now I'm sitting comfortably, so tell me everything before I die of curiosity.'

As succinctly as possible, Charlotte explained about the

storm and the car breaking down. 'But luckily we were close to one of the estate cottages, so Simon suggested that we spend the night there.'

'Ooh, the devil! Were you alone?'

'Yes.'

'Share a bed?'

'Yes.'

'No regrets?'

'None. Even before he proposed.'

'That's wonderful,' Sojo said slowly.

'But?'

'I can't help but worry in case this is just on the rebound from Wudolf. Because if it is—'

'It isn't,' Charlotte broke in decisively. 'As you yourself said, Rudy's very Byronic, and I was on the verge of being infatuated, but that's all...'

'So it won't rock the boat if I let on that he rang this morning wanting to speak to you?' Sojo revealed.

'No, it won't. What did you tell him?'

'That you were away for the weekend, but just in case he had the nerve to ring Farringdon Hall, I didn't say where.'

Charlotte breathed a sigh of relief.

'I hope I did the right thing?' her flatmate asked.

'Yes. I wouldn't have wanted him to ring here.'

'Knowing how painfully honest you are, I suppose you'll want to put him in the picture. What will you do? Ring him up, or write to him?'

'I can't do either,' Charlotte said. 'I don't know his home address or his phone number, or where to contact him in New York.'

'Well, if he hasn't got fed up and stopped ringing before I get back, I'll be pleased to tell him that you're going to marry someone far nicer. Incidentally, I'd love to see his face,' Sojo said naughtily.

'I hope he won't be hurt,' Charlotte remarked a shade anxiously.

'Don't start feeling guilty. The only thing likely to be hurt is his pride. I know his sort. That's why I'm glad you're not still hankering after him... You aren't, are you?'

'No, not in the slightest. In retrospect I can see that I wasn't in love with him. I'm not sure I even liked him.'

'What about Simon? Are you in love with him? Or is that a question I shouldn't ask?'

'Ask it by all means. The answer is *madly*. I was lost the moment I saw him. A *coup de foudre*.'

'And it was mutual, I take it?'

'Yes.'

Sojo sighed. 'How romantic. But to get to the nitty-gritty, does Sir Nigel know?'

'Yes, we told him almost as soon as we got back.'

'What did he say?'

'For some reason he seems to have taken a fancy to me, and he was genuinely pleased. He's going to give me away.'

'I thought he was very ill,' Sojo commented.

'He is. That's why Simon would like us to get married as soon as possible. He's going to apply for a special licence so we can arrange the wedding for Wednesday or Thursday.'

'You don't mean *this* Wednesday or Thursday?' Sojo asked faintly.

'Yes...'

'Well, he certainly doesn't waste any time.'

'And I'd like you to be my bridesmaid.'

'I was only joking, you know,' Sojo protested laughingly.

'I'm not.'

'What does Simon think of the idea?'

'He suggested it.'

'Then I'd love to! I'll dig out my best frock.'

'Speaking of frocks, I'd be grateful if you could pack my clothes and shoes et cetera and bring them down with you.'

'All of them?'

'I suppose so. I won't be coming back.'

'Of course you won't.' Just for a moment she sounded lost. 'I'm afraid it hasn't sunk in yet. Do you mind if I keep the flat on? It's become home.'

'Of course I don't mind. I was hoping you would.'

'What about the shop?'

'I'm going to ask Margaret if she'll manage it, at least for the time being,' Charlotte said.

'She once told me she felt far too young to retire, so it's my bet she would be happy to manage it on a permanent basis. I don't suppose you're planning to work after you're married?'

'I haven't even thought that far ahead. But I can't imagine Simon would want me to.'

'Aah…'

'What do you mean, aah…?'

'You used to be so cool and self-sufficient. Now, I'm delighted to say, your voice goes all soppy every time you say *Simon.*'

'It does no such thing,' Charlotte protested.

Taking the denial for what it was worth, Sojo added, 'I can't wait to meet the man who's had such a devastating effect on you, so I'll grab a sandwich and get cracking with the packing. See ya!'

The line went dead.

Smiling to herself, Charlotte pressed *end call* and tapped in Margaret's number.

When the older woman had heard the news, after a flurry of oohs and aahs and excited congratulations, she expressed her willingness to manage the shop for as long as Charlotte wanted her to.

'It's all happened so quickly,' she added, 'I can hardly believe it.'

Charlotte felt very much the same.

'Fancy being swept off your feet like that!' She sighed gustily. 'Isn't it wonderfully romantic? I hope you'll both live happily ever after, just like they do in fairy tales...'

But were fairy tales bound to have happy endings? Charlotte wondered as she replaced the receiver.

Not necessarily. She recalled a poetic version of *Spellbound* that ended, *'glass coffin, no prince.'*

Despite the warmth of the room, a sudden cold chill, a *premonition*, drained the colour from her face and made a shiver run through her.

'Is there a problem?' Simon's voice asked.

Feeling silly, she said, 'No... No, everything's fine. Sojo seems highly delighted, and Margaret is quite willing to manage the shop for as long as I want her to.'

'Then why are you looking so upset?'

She managed a smile. 'I'm not.'

Plainly dissatisfied, he was about to probe further when there was a tap at the door and Mrs Reynolds appeared, to say, 'Lunch is ready when you are. It being Sunday, I've asked Milly to set it in the dining-room. I hope that's all right?'

'Yes, fine. Thank you, Ann.'

A hand at Charlotte's waist, he ushered her through to the panelled dining-room, where a table that would have held a dozen or more was set for two.

'So what's wrong?' he pursued, when they were seated and the soup had been served.

'Nothing's wrong, really.'

Seeing a frown draw his well-marked brows together, she added awkwardly, 'It was just that Margaret said she hoped we would both live happily ever after, ''like they do in fairy tales''. I was just wondering if fairy tales always ended happily, when a goose walked over my grave…'

He looked oddly relieved.

Eager to change the subject, she asked, 'How did you get on?'

'I had a word with both Matthew and James. They were pleased to hear the news. James is quite willing to be best man, and Matthew said he could see no reason why, if the vicar of our chosen church was agreeable, we shouldn't start planning the wedding for Wednesday. Unfortunately he's away at a conference and won't be able to attend, but, bearing in mind Grandfather's state of health, he agreed that the ceremony should take place as soon as possible. As luck would have it, I was able to catch the Reverend David Moss, the vicar of St Peter's, between his morning service and lunch. He had nothing scheduled for Wednesday, so I've arranged for an eleven o'clock wedding, if that's all right by you?'

'Fine.'

'Then that's the most important thing settled,' he said with satisfaction.

An odd little shiver ran though her, leaving her shaken and uncertain. She *wanted* to marry Simon, *wanted* to be his wife, so why, instead of feeling joyful and happy, did she feel uneasy, as if some sixth sense was warning that all was not well?

'Which leaves just a few odd ends to tie in,' he went on. 'The most important of which is a decision on where you'd like to spend your first honeymoon. I suggested Paris or Rome as being reasonably close—we can always go further afield at a later date—but if there's anywhere else you prefer…Amsterdam? Venice? Vienna?'

She shook her head. 'I'm quite happy with either Paris or Rome.'

'It's for you to choose.'

'Then Rome. Along with some student friends I spent a weekend in Paris, which I loved, but I've never been to Rome.'

'Rather than staying in the city itself, which can be extremely noisy, I suggest that we find somewhere in the hills just outside Rome. There are some delightful little villages...'

While they discussed the various options, she made a determined effort to dismiss the feeling of uneasiness. But a faint niggle persisted until lunch was over.

As they left the dining-room, he asked, 'Are you planning to let your mother and stepfather know about the wedding?'

'I'm afraid I hadn't thought about it,' she admitted. 'Though I will, of course.'

'Perhaps you'd like to phone them now?'

Well aware that the *suddenness* would come as a shock to her conservative mother, Charlotte hesitated. Then realising they *had* to know, and it would be as well to get it over with, she said, 'If you don't mind?'

'Of course not. By the way, what's your mother's name now she's remarried?'

'Harris. Joan Harris. Her husband's called Steve.'

Simon glanced at his watch. 'Do they stay up late?'

'I don't really know.'

'Well, it will be getting on for midnight in Sydney. Do you want to see if you can catch them?'

'Please.'

CHAPTER SEVEN

HE LED the way to the library, which was a large, handsome room with book-lined walls and an elaborately decorated plaster ceiling.

There was a soft leather suite and a Turkey red carpet with matching velvet curtains held back by tasselled cords. Though the day had remained sunny, a cheerful log fire burned in the wide grate.

In front of the window an imposing leather-topped desk, with a matching chair, held all the latest state-of-the-art office equipment. Sitting down at the desk, Charlotte dialled her parents' number.

When, after a short delay, her mother answered, she blurted out, 'Mum, it's me.'

'It's very late to ring. Is there something wrong?' Joan asked, her voice concerned.

'No, there's nothing wrong. Just the opposite. I know it's a bit late, but I wanted to give you the good news without delay. I'm getting married.'

Quickly, before the questions started to flow, Charlotte told her mother the relevant details.

'This Wednesday!' Joan sounded staggered. 'It's all so sudden. Why didn't you tell us sooner?'

'Well, everything's happened quite quickly and—'

'But I've never even heard you mention anyone called Simon.'

Somewhat hampered by Simon's presence, Charlotte said carefully, 'We haven't known each other all that long. You might say it was love at first sight—'

Only when the words were out did she realise it was the wrong thing to say.

Sounding even more anxious, Joan broke in, 'I've always mistrusted that kind of thing. Too often it's just infatuation. Love should have time to grow.'

'Normally I would agree with you but—'

'Surely it would be a lot wiser to wait a while and give it some thought?' Joan insisted.

'Simon doesn't want to wait, you see—'

'As you don't *have* to get married...' Then, obviously horrified by the idea, she cried, 'You don't, do you? You're not pregnant?'

Feeling guilty because she could so easily be, Charlotte said, 'No, of course not.'

Joan breathed a sigh of relief. 'Then it would be a big mistake to rush into things. My advice is, take your time.'

'We haven't much time. You see, Simon would like his grandfather, who is terminally ill, to be present at the wedding, and—'

'But we don't know a thing about this Simon; we haven't even set eyes on him. You might be making a terrible mistake, and you know what they say—marry in haste, repent at leisure...'

Seeing the hunted look on Charlotte's face, Simon took the phone off her and said quietly, 'Mrs Harris, this is Simon Farringdon. I realise the suddenness must have come as something of a shock for you, and I do apologise. However, all the arrangements are in place, and things will be going ahead as planned—'

'I do think you should—'

'It would give us great pleasure if you and your husband could get over for the wedding,' Simon cut in smoothly. 'And we'd be delighted if you would be our guests at Farringdon Hall.'

'As it's such short notice, I—'

'There's no need to worry about arranging flights; I'll be happy to send the company jet for you.'

'How very kind,' she said faintly. 'But I don't think...' Then in a rush, 'To tell you the truth, I'm frightened to death of flying. Just the thought makes me ill—'

'That's a great pity, but we do understand.'

His voice holding a polite but decided finality, he added, 'Now, as it's so late, we'd better wish you goodnight. I'm sure Charlotte will fill you in on all the details when we get back from our honeymoon.'

He replaced the receiver, before asking half-jokingly, 'How on earth did you survive?'

'She loves me. It's just that she's always been overly concerned about me.'

'So much concern must have been a little bit wearisome.'

'Dad diluted it somewhat, and shortly after he died I went away to college.'

'That must have been a relief.'

'It was,' she admitted. 'Though at the time I felt terribly disloyal.'

He raised a level brow. 'Why was that?'

'Because I was one of the lucky ones,' she said quietly. 'Some of my fellow students had no one who cared, and everyone needs someone to love them and be concerned about them.'

A strange look flitted across his face, but before she could decipher it, it was gone.

Rising to his feet, he suggested, 'Perhaps you'd like to take a look at the books, while I go and put Grandfather in the picture?'

Books had always been a pleasure to her and for the next fifteen minutes or so, putting aside the slight feeling of agitation caused by the phone call, she browsed happily.

She was sitting on the couch, a seventeenth-century volume open on her lap, when Simon returned. Coming over to sit by her side, he took her left hand and slipped a ring onto her fourth finger.

A single magnificent diamond in a simple gold setting, it fitted perfectly.

'This was my mother's, but if you don't like it please don't hesitate to say so, and tomorrow we'll look for something else.'

'It's absolutely beautiful,' she said huskily, and lifted her face for his kiss.

Instead of kissing her, however, with an almost business-like air, he took a slim leather case from his pocket and flicked it open with his thumb nail.

On the blue velvet lining lay a thin gold chain with an exquisite, many-faceted diamond 'teardrop' that seemed to sparkle with an inner fire.

She caught her breath.

'It would please Grandfather enormously if you would wear this on your wedding day.'

'Is it a family heirloom?'

'In a manner of speaking. In the early fifteen-hundreds it was given to Carlotta Bell-Farringdon by an Italian noble-man who was madly in love with her. Since then it's been known as the Carlotta Stone, and, as Carlotta is the Italian form of Charlotte, it seems very fitting.'

Charlotte reached the stone gently. 'It's beautiful and I'd love to wear it,' she said.

'Ah, this appears to be Miss Macfadyen arriving.'

Following his gaze through the leaded window-panes Charlotte saw a grey chauffeur-driven limousine was just drawing up on the gravel apron.

'If you want to go and meet her…?' He closed the jewel case with a snap. 'I'll just lock this away before I join you.'

As she made to take off the ring, he said, 'No, leave that on. I'd like you to wear it.'

A smile on her lips, Charlotte hurried outside to see Sojo

descending from the car with all the panache of visiting royalty.

Her blonde hair had been newly washed and tamed into a shining, two-layered, shoulder-length bob. She was dressed up to the nines in her best jade-green trouser suit and a trailing scarf of the type that strangled Isadora Duncan.

While the chauffeur lifted out the luggage, her gaze ranging over the Hall, she exclaimed, 'Imagine you living in a place like this…!'

Then, catching sight of Charlotte's ring, 'Wowee! Just look at the size of that rock! A family heirloom at a guess?'

'It belonged to Simon's mother.'

'Do you know I'm black and blue? I've been pinching myself all the way here just to make absolutely sure I wasn't dreaming.'

'I must admit I've felt like doing the same,' Charlotte confessed. 'Everything's happened so fast.'

'You're not kidding! By the way, the two big cases are full of your stuff. I've packed everything I could find, but if I've missed anything—'

'Don't worry, if it's at all important I can always collect it later.'

'Of course.' Sojo looked relieved. 'It's just that when you said you wouldn't be coming back, it sounded so final…'

Simon, who had joined them unnoticed, held out his hand. 'Welcome to Farringdon Hall, Miss Macfadyen… I'm Simon Farringdon.'

He smiled at her, a smile that trebled his already powerful sex appeal.

Just for a second or two she goggled at him, then, recovering her poise, she shook his hand and said politely, 'It's nice to meet you, Mr Farringdon.'

Leading the way into the hall, he suggested, 'I think it

would be a good idea if we skipped the formalities and went on to first-name terms.'

Straight-faced, he suggested, 'If you call me Simon, I'll call you Sojourner.'

'You will not! Or if you do, it'll be at your peril!' Then, seeing the gleam of devilment in his green-gold eyes, she grinned broadly. 'I see Charlotte has already put you in the picture.'

'How do you come to have such an *interesting* name?' he asked blandly.

'An aberration on my mother's part.' Darkly, she added, 'Parents who give innocent little children *interesting* names have a lot to answer for.'

He acknowledged the riposte before saying, 'I tend to agree with you. Where did she get Sojourner from?'

'She'd just finished reading a novel called *Southwest of Georgia*. Would you believe she still can't see what she did to me?'

'Sojourner's not *that* bad,' Charlotte protested.

'Go wash your mouth out with soap and water.'

At that instant Mrs Reynolds appeared.

A smile playing around his lips, Simon said, 'Ann, this is Miss Macfadyen.'

'It's nice to meet you, Miss Macfadyen,' the housekeeper greeted the newcomer cheerfully. 'I've put you next door to Miss Christie. If you'd care to follow me, Martin will bring the luggage up.'

Sojo glanced at Charlotte, who, interpreting that silent plea, offered, 'I'll come with you so we can have a chat while you get settled in.'

'When you girls come down I'll be in the library,' Simon told them. Then to Mrs Reynolds, 'If you're not too busy, Ann, perhaps we could have some tea?'

'Certainly.'

It was obvious that he could do no wrong in the housekeeper's eyes, and if he'd asked for the moon she would have done her best to provide it.

When the luggage had been brought up and the two girls were alone, Sojo, who had been obviously simmering, burst out excitedly, 'Isn't he just something! My fingers were itching to sketch him. Those eyes and that mouth—' she shivered deliciously '—and those *shoulders*... He makes Wudolf look like an immature schoolboy.'

'I thought you fancied Rudy?' Charlotte teased.

'*I* thought I did at the time. It just goes to show what a dearth of personable men there's been in my life over the past couple of years.'

While Sojo unpacked her case, she continued to wax lyrical. 'I find it most inspiring to know that men as gorgeous as Simon Farringdon do still exist. Though they're obviously few and far between, so my chances of actually meeting one must be pretty slim,' she added gloomily.

Then, brightening, 'Still, it's nice to feel the old libido stirring again.'

Hiding a smile, Charlotte queried, 'Do I gather you fancy him?'

'Like mad. He has enough sex appeal to set fire to a swamp,' her friend declared.

'But do you *like* him?' Charlotte asked.

'Yes, I do.' Sojo's answer was unequivocal. 'Not only is he one of the most attractive men I've ever met, but even more important, he seems genuinely *nice*. I like the way he treats his staff. He's also mature in a way that Wudolf never will be. If things didn't go his way I can't imagine Simon acting like a petulant child. Mind you, having said he's nice, I don't mean weak in any way. I imagine, if justified, he could be quite formidable. Not a man to cross swords with...'

The last of her things put away, she said enthusiastically,

'Right. Ready when you are. Let me go and take another look at this idol, see if I can spot any feet of clay.'

'I rather hope you can,' Charlotte told her half seriously. 'Perfection must be terribly hard to live up to.'

While they descended the stairs Sojo gazed around her with wide-eyed admiration. 'If I asked him nicely, do you think he might find time to show me round the old ancestral home?'

'I'm sure he will. He seems to genuinely love Farringdon Hall.'

'What about you?'

'It's already starting to feel like home,' Charlotte said simply.

Satisfied, Sojo nodded.

When they reached the library, Simon rose from behind his desk and joined them in front of the fire.

Waiting on the low table was a tray that held everything needed for tea, including dainty sandwiches and buttered scones.

As soon as the two women were seated side by side on the settee, Simon reached for the silver teapot and began to pour.

Sojo's sigh of relief was audible.

He glanced at her, one eyebrow raised.

'I dread the question, *who's going to be mother?*'

The phrase was delivered in such mincing tones that Simon threw back his head and laughed. 'Do people still say that?'

'One of my boyfriends did. That's why he's an ex.'

'Milk and sugar?'

'Just milk, please.'

'Speaking of boyfriends,' Simon pursued, 'I hope this invitation hasn't ruffled any male feathers?'

'Nary a one. I've gone off men for the moment.'

'Any particular reason?'

'The last two have been nerds.'

'Oh? In what way?' Simon asked interestedly.

As though wondering if she was hogging the conversation, Sojo glanced at her friend.

But, only too happy that the liking appeared to be mutual, and the pair were getting on so well, Charlotte was content to sit back and listen.

Seeing this, Sojo continued, 'Mark, the latest, was totally boring. He had only one thing on his mind, and hands like Velcro.'

His face straight, Simon commented, 'A very descriptive phrase. What about the previous one?'

'He didn't live in the real world. Mind you, with a name like Tarquin, who could blame him? Thank you...'

When she and Charlotte had both accepted a cup of tea and a plate, Simon drew the table closer so they could help themselves. Then, his tawny eyes sparkling with laughter, Simon remarked, 'I can quite see why you've gone off men.'

'Not *all* men.' An inveterate flirt, she fluttered her new false eyelashes at him shamelessly.

'I'm flattered,' he assured her gravely. 'Though I'd rather like to know why I'm an exception.'

'Well, for one thing you're obviously good for Charlotte. I've never seen her look so happy...'

Just for a split-second he appeared to be disconcerted, then his expression cleared, and, one eyebrow raised, he queried, 'And?'

'And I wondered, if I said *pretty please*, if you would show me round the Hall some time?'

'I'd be delighted.'

'Providing, of course, that you're not too busy running the Bell-Farringdon business empire?'

So Sojo had been checking up, Charlotte thought, and hoped Simon wouldn't mind.

But he was answering calmly, 'From now until the wedding's over I'm leaving Michael Forrester, my right-hand man, to deal with everything and taking a complete break.'

'Wonder of wonders! A top businessman who's willing to delegate.'

'I admit to having been a workaholic in the past, but no longer. From now on I intend to work much shorter hours. I want time to relax and have fun, time to spend with my wife and family.'

Sojo gave Charlotte a speaking glance. *Didn't I tell you a man of his class would want a family to inherit things?* Aloud, she remarked, 'That sounds too good to be true.'

'Not a bit of it. I've started as I mean to go on... Now, if you've finished your tea I'd be pleased to give you the Grand Tour. That is, if Charlotte doesn't have any objections?'

'Of course not,' Charlotte said. 'In fact I'd love to come with you.'

'Then we'll leave the Long Gallery until last, and I'll point out the more interesting portraits.'

Apparently stunned by the height and grandeur of the Great Chamber, and the beauty of the house itself, Sojo followed in awed silence while Simon provided a wealth of interesting historical details.

Finally, he remarked, 'Well, that's about it; apart from the Long Gallery, which is on your right, you've seen all the rooms of any interest.'

Sounding disappointed, Sojo asked, 'Don't you have a haunted room?'

'Not really.'

'But surely you have a ghost?' she persisted hopefully.

'Not one you need worry about,' he said smoothly.

'Oh, I'm not worried. Just fascinated.' She gave an excited wriggle. 'There's nothing I enjoy more than a nice spooky ghost.'

Simon laughed. 'Sorry to disappoint you, but it isn't the kind that wanders about moaning and rattling its chains.'

'What does it do?' Then, aware she must have appeared flippant, she said quickly, 'I'm sorry, I didn't mean that like it sounded. What I meant to ask is, what *kind* of ghost is it? Someone who was walled up? An ancestor who died in battle?'

He shook his head. 'Nothing so exciting, I'm afraid. If it exists at all, it's just the spirit of a young girl...'

As they turned into the Long Gallery, he invited ironically, 'Come and meet the ancestors.'

Gazing at the portraits in amazement, Sojo asked, 'Do all these belong to the Farringdon family?'

'Most of them are of the bloodline, the others are in-laws.'

As they paused in front of the portrait of a handsome, dark-haired man with a short, pointed beard, a luxuriant moustache and a rakish air, Sojo commented, 'Now, *he* looks as though he could have been a bit of a lad.'

'That's a pretty fair assessment.' Turning to Charlotte, Simon asked, 'Can you guess who he is?'

'Sir Roger Farringdon?'

'Got it in one.'

'Better known as the queen's favourite,' Charlotte added.

'Why was that?' Sojo asked innocently.

When Simon had explained, they strolled on while he named various people and gave brief details of their role in the family.

'Who's that?' Sojo enquired, pointing to a picture of a beautiful young girl with high cheekbones and a passionate mouth. Her black hair was taken up into an elaborate chignon, and she was wearing a gold brocade evening gown and a magnificent teardrop diamond around her swan-like neck.

'That's Carlotta Bell-Farringdon,' Simon answered.

'I must say that's some rock she's wearing…if it's real?'

'Oh, yes, it's real enough.'

As Sojo's eyes widened, he explained, 'The diamond was given to her by her lover, who was the descendant of a doge known as the Lion of Venice. It's come to be called the Carlotta Stone.'

'Did she and her lover marry?'

'Unfortunately they weren't able to. He already had a wife.'

'So she died an old maid pining for him?'

'Not at all. Shortly after the portrait was painted she married the Duke of Cessina.'

As they neared the end of the gallery, indicating three portraits by Samuel Launston, he said, 'That's Sophia and Joshua, my great-grandparents, and the young man next to them is Grandfather when he was twenty-one.'

'I would have known,' Charlotte said. 'Other than getting older, Sir Nigel hasn't altered all that much. He's still a nice-looking man.'

'Now, that's strange…' Leaning forward, Sojo was studying the portrait intently.

'Strange in what way?' Simon queried.

'The young girl there, the delicate-looking one…she's very like Charlotte.'

His expression impassive, Simon said nothing.

Returning her gaze to the picture, Sojo pursued, 'She has the same-shaped eyes… And look at her ears… See what I mean? Small and neat, hardly any lobes? Just like Charlotte's.'

She turned to Charlotte and, only half joking, asked, 'You were adopted, weren't you? So it's possible you're related to the girl in this picture in some way.'

Feeling uncomfortable, Charlotte said crisply, 'The very idea's ridiculous.'

Sojo sighed. 'As I've said before, you have no sense of the dramatic.'

'You're very good at spotting a likeness.' Simon observed admiringly.

'A trained eye. Ever since I was able to hold a pencil I've sketched people. I spent a year at art school, hoping to become an artist, but it didn't work out... So who is she?'

Glancing at Charlotte, Simon asked, 'Who do *you* think she is?'

Gazing at the small, heart-shaped face, its childish beauty framed by a cloud of dark, silky hair, she ventured, 'Mara?'

He nodded. As they moved on, turning to Sojo, he explained, 'Grandfather had twin sisters. Mara was the younger one. She died when she was seven.'

'And she's your ghost?' Sojo guessed shrewdly.

'In a manner of speaking.'

'Does she still haunt the place?'

'No, I don't believe she does. Though perhaps her spirit lingered for a while. Who knows?'

'Sounds fascinating. Tell me more.'

'I will over dinner tonight. I'm taking the pair of you to dance and dine at Rumplestiltskins.'

Fluttering her eyelashes at him, Sojo asked audaciously, 'I take it there's no chance of the car breaking down again on the way back?'

Simon looked at Charlotte.

As her cheeks grow hot and her grey eyes fell beneath that ironic gaze, he answered lightly, ''Fraid not. If there's one thing I've learnt, it's never to use the same ruse twice.'

The last portrait was of a couple. A man who had an unmistakable look of Sir Nigel, and a flaxen-haired woman with tawny-green eyes whose face, rather than being merely pretty, was strong and full of character. She was wearing the ring that now graced Charlotte's finger.

'Your parents,' Charlotte said to Simon with certainty.

'Yes. As you can see, I take after my mother.'

'I was wondering how you came to be blond,' Sojo remarked, 'when most of the Farringdons seem to have dark
hair.'

As they left the gallery behind them, she added, 'Well,
thank you for the Grand Tour. I've really enjoyed it.'

'My pleasure. Now, suppose you and Charlotte go and
get your best bib and tucker on, and I'll see you in the hall
in about half an hour.'

'It'll have to be my second best. I'm saving my best dress
for the wedding,' Sojo teased.

'There's no need. Tuesday I'll be taking the pair of you
to town to shop for your wedding finery.'

'You don't mean…?'

'Ring, bridal gown and veil, bridesmaid's dress, accessories, the lot,' Simon stated.

'It just gets better. Have you anything lined up for tomorrow?' Sojo asked.

'Tomorrow we'll need to make all the arrangements for
Wednesday. Cars, catering, bridal flowers, church flowers,
an organist, someone to take photographs, last minute in-
vitations, et cetera…'

'Can it all be put in place in such a short time?' Charlotte
wanted to know.

'Certainly it can.'

'Money comes in handy, I dare say,' Sojo twinkled up at
him.

'It can be used to grease a few palms where necessary,'
he agreed, quite unruffled. 'But your practical help will be
even more useful.'

Sojo beamed with pleasure. 'I really do love weddings! I
haven't had this much fun since my sister got married.'

The wedding morning dawned clear and bright, a golden
September day, warm and welcome as a blessing. To avoid

the media descending on them, they had done their best to keep the whole thing a secret. Nothing had been put in the papers, and there was to be no official photographer.

Following tradition, Simon kept out of the way while the girls—Sojo, bubbling with excitement, Charlotte a little quiet, but both conscious that things would never be quite the same again—prepared for the wedding.

When Sojo had helped Charlotte put on a deceptively simple ivory silk dress and a matching circlet that went round her dark chignon and held her short veil in place, she stood back to admire her handiwork.

'Well, all I can say is, Simon's a very lucky man.'

With a grin, she added, 'Discreet too. Though I'm right next door at nights I've never heard so much as a latch click.'

'There's been nothing to hear,' Charlotte said.

'*You* went to *his* room?' the other girl asked.

'We both stayed put.'

'Your choice?'

Charlotte shook her head. It hadn't been her choice. If Simon had lifted a finger, she would have gone running. But since the wedding arrangements had been made he had barely touched her, let alone kissed her. Although he had laughed and joked with Sojo, he had treated *her* with a kind of distant courteousness that was somehow chilling.

A tap at the door interrupted her thoughts.

It was Mrs Reynolds bringing two Cellophane boxes containing the flowers, and a message asking if Charlotte could spare a moment to see Sir Nigel.

'Of course,' Charlotte agreed, and hastened along the corridor, her skirts sweeping the floorboards.

Having refused any medication that might make him sleepy, and sent his nurse packing until he called for her, Sir Nigel was already dressed and seated in a wheelchair, a cream carnation in his buttonhole.

He studied Charlotte for a moment, then, his eyes growing misty, he said, 'In true Bell-Farringdon tradition, you make a beautiful bride.'

She smiled at him shakily. 'Thank you, Sir Nigel.'

'No more of that *Sir Nigel* stuff. From now on I'd like you to call me Grandfather. Go on, let me hear you say it.'

'Thank you, Grandfather.'

He smiled at her. 'That's my girl. It's going to be a great day. My only regret is that Simon's sister can't be here.'

'I was very sorry to hear about Lucy's accident,' Charlotte said sincerely. 'It must have been a big worry for you all.'

'Thank you, my dear. It has been pretty grim.'

'How did it happen?' she asked.

'She and her husband had just left the hotel they'd been dining at, when their car clipped another one, went off the road and rolled down an embankment. It was towards the end of March and bitterly cold. There was black ice... Luckily the driver of the other car was uninjured.'

'Was her husband...?'

'He got off practically scot-free, just cuts and bruises—' there was bitterness in the old man's voice '—whereas Lucy suffered severe internal and spinal injuries. Not only did she lose her baby, but also the hope of having any more.'

Shocked, Charlotte breathed, 'How *awful* for her.'

'Would you like a family?' he wanted to know.

'Yes, I would.'

He smiled. 'I'm delighted. It means the Bell-Farringdon bloodline will go on.'

'That's important to you,' Charlotte realised.

Though it was a statement not a question, he answered, 'Yes, my dear, it is. Very important.'

'I'm truly sorry about Lucy...'

'It was a blow to us all,' he admitted. 'With losing their parents so young, Simon and his sister have always been very close. He'd do anything to make her happy. When she fell in love with a man we both thought was worthless and unprincipled, Simon tried hard to talk her out of marrying him. But she was quite determined, and in the end they ran off and got married at a register office. After that we had no choice but to make the best of it for Lucy's sake...'

Charlotte had just decided Sir Nigel wasn't going to say any more when, frowning a little, he went on, 'When they'd been married a few months, she said he was getting restless and asked Simon to give him a job. Rather than see him live off Lucy's money, Simon agreed, and, never a man to do things by halves, put him in a position of trust. I believe he's regretted it since. By the way, he mentioned that you would have asked Lucy to be one of your attendants. It was very thoughtful of you, and I'm quite sure that she and Miss Macfadyen would have got on well.'

Catching Charlotte's look of surprise, he added, 'I like your friend. She shares the same kind of spirited, yet down-to-earth, approach to life that Lucy has...' His face clouding, he added, 'Or *had* before the accident.'

Then, perking up, 'But the latest news is good. The doctors believe there's a fair chance she'll be out of bed and starting to walk again by the new year, so we have a lot to be thankful for. Now, my dear, time's getting short, and, as it's supposed to be unlucky for the groom to see the bride before they get to church, I thought you might allow me to put this on.'

He held up the Carlotta Stone.

She went down on her knees by his chair and, after a brief struggle, he fastened the chain around her neck and slipped home the safety catch.

'There!' he said with satisfaction. 'It looks well on you.'

Touching it, she began, 'I'll take great care of it and return it as soon as—'

'I don't want it back,' he said firmly. 'I want you to keep it.'

'Oh, b-but I couldn't possibly,' she stammered.

'I insist.'

'Shouldn't Lucy—?'

'Apart from the fact that Lucy is a rich woman in her own right, she has her mother's jewels,' Sir Nigel said.

'But what will Simon say?'

'I've already discussed it with him and he agrees that you should have it.'

She made another attempt. 'But apart from the fact that it must be priceless, it's a family heirloom. Suppose something happened—?'

Shaking his head, he broke in decidedly, 'Whatever happens, my dear, the Carlotta Stone is yours to keep, and Simon fully approves. Now, off you go, and I'll see you downstairs as soon as they've finished putting the chairlift in place.'

CHAPTER EIGHT

FEELING more than a little dazed, Charlotte made her way back to the bedroom, where Sojo was looking her best in a claret-coloured silk dress with a matching headband and shoes.

When the blonde caught sight of the diamond, her jaw dropped. 'That looks like the Carlotta Stone.'

'It is,' Charlotte revealed.

'I hope it's a copy, otherwise we'll need a church full of bodyguards.'

'It isn't.'

'Bet you'll be glad to hand it safely back,' Sojo said knowingly.

'Sir Nigel insisted on giving it to me.'

'Say that again?' The look on Sojo's face was priceless.

'Sir Nigel insisted on giving it to me. He said he'd discussed it with Simon, and whatever happened it was mine to keep,' Charlotte said.

'Crikey! How does it feel to own a bauble that could almost pay off the national debt?'

'I'm not sure,' Charlotte admitted uneasily. 'I still haven't quite taken it in.'

'And your engagement ring must be worth a small fortune... By the way, speaking as an experienced bridesmaid, you'll need to move it to your right hand to leave space for your wedding ring.'

As Charlotte obeyed, Sojo remarked with immense satisfaction, 'It's just like a fairy story, the way you've moved from rags to riches in so short a time.'

Sighing gustily, she added, 'I just love the Cinderella-Rockefeller-type romance, don't you?'

'I used to at one time,' Charlotte agreed. 'Now I find the role of Cinderella is anything but comfortable. I didn't even buy my own wedding dress.'

'Did you want to get married in some cast-off from a charity shop?' Sojo exclaimed.

'No, but I would have felt happier in something I'd paid for myself,' Charlotte admitted quietly.

'Lord give me strength! You're starting to talk like Jane Eyre. You know, I've always felt sorry for Mr Rochester. Jane was so strait-laced and gloomy.'

'I don't mean to seem ungrateful, but it makes me feel at a disadvantage,' Charlotte insisted.

'There's something wrong with you. Most women would give their eye-teeth to be in your position. Me included. And I wouldn't necessarily put money, or the Carlotta Stone, as the main incentive...'

There was a tap at the door, and Mrs Reynolds put her head round to announce that the wedding cars had duly arrived.

'Thanks,' Sojo said. 'I'll be right there.'

Turning to Charlotte, she ordered, 'Now then, be happy,' and hugged her with an unexpected show of emotion, before gathering up her posy of wine-red roses and hurrying downstairs.

When, five minutes later, Charlotte picked up her own dainty bouquet of ivory lilies and followed her down, she found Sir Nigel waiting for her in a car specially adapted to take a wheelchair.

Smiling at him, she gathered her skirts and climbed in to sit beside him.

During the short journey to the church, he took her hand and said, 'You'll never know how happy you've made me.'

She leaned to kiss the papery cheek that smelled faintly of eau-de-Cologne and aftershave. 'I'm so glad you don't mind. It all happened so fast...'

'You do love my grandson, don't you?'

'Yes,' she said simply.

'I was certain of it, and I'm only too delighted that everything's worked out and you and Simon are getting married.'

The words coming out in a rush, she said, 'During the past two or three days he's seemed a little distant… unapproachable…especially when we were alone. I couldn't help but wonder if he might have changed his mind.'

'Believe me, if he had he would have said so. No, I'm sure he loves you…'

She breathed a sigh of relief and happiness. There had been moments when she had been sure he didn't even *like* her, let alone *love* her.

'But in his own way he's a stickler for propriety, which must seem a bit of an anachronism in this modern age where anything goes. Still, he's one of the finest men I know, and I'm quite convinced that he'll make a good husband, and that you and he will be very happy together.'

Patting the hand he was still holding, Sir Nigel added, 'When you come back from your honeymoon we'll have a long talk and set everything straight…really get to know one another.'

When they reached St Peter's to find no trace of the Press, Sir Nigel looked relieved. 'We seem to have been successful in keeping the newshounds in the dark. I was concerned that in spite of all our efforts they might have got wind of the wedding and be waiting… Now then, my dear, all set?'

'All set.'

The driver pushing the wheelchair, they made their way through the lych-gate and up the yew-bordered path to the main door, where the Reverend David Moss was waiting for them.

The old church was full of sunshine and sound and colour, with organ music bursting out joyously, masses of scented flowers, and streamers of bejewelled light cast by the stained-glass windows.

A handful of villagers, mainly relatives of the estate workers, were seated in the pews, dressed in their Sunday best.

Simon, strikingly handsome in pearl-grey, a cream carnation in his buttonhole, was waiting, his expression austere. The best man, who took his duties seriously, stood at his shoulder, a look of concentration on his fair face.

At a signal from the vicar, the organist changed from Bach to Saint-Saëns and Charlotte walked up the aisle beside Sir Nigel, her hand in his, while Sojo pushed the wheelchair.

Of the small wedding party, Sir Nigel and Sojo looked by far the happiest.

As Charlotte handed over her bouquet and took her place by Simon's side, he turned his head to look at her. Buoyed up by her conversation with Sir Nigel, she smiled at him.

There was no answering smile.

His failure to respond shrivelled her happiness like a frost shrivelled the bright autumn leaves.

The vicar cleared his throat and began, 'Dearly beloved, we are gathered together here...'

As the short, simple service progressed, and Simon never even glanced at her, Charlotte wondered afresh if he was regretting it.

'Wilt thou have this woman to thy wedded wife...?'

She listened, her whole attention concentrated painfully on Simon's responses.

If she was expecting any hesitation, any trace of regret or uncertainty, she found none. He answered decisively, as though he knew exactly what he was doing, and had every intention of doing it.

Slightly reassured, she made her own vows quietly but clearly.

When he had placed the plain gold ring on her fourth

finger and they were declared man and wife, in response to the vicar's, 'You may now kiss the bride,' he bent his head and kissed her lightly on the lips.

There was nothing lover-like about it. He could almost have been kissing someone he didn't particularly like, out of a sense of duty.

When the service was over, before leading the way into the vestry to sign the marriage certificate, the vicar, on Sir Nigel's behalf, invited the small congregation to a reception at the Hall, assuring them of lifts there and back.

Once in the vestry, Charlotte was hugged and kissed and told she looked beautiful. Everyone congratulated Simon and shook his hand, except for Sojo, who stood on tiptoe to kiss him while Sir Nigel looked on, smiling benignly.

As soon as the formalities were completed the wedding party made their way out into the sunshine, where one of the estate workers, an amateur photographer, was waiting with his camera.

With a tremendous effort of will, Sir Nigel stood, leaning on his grandson's arm and smiling broadly, while a series of photographs were taken.

Keen to do a good job, the photographer would have gone on to take more, but, indicating that enough was enough, Simon thanked him, before helping his grandfather back into the wheelchair.

Then, accompanied by the bride and groom, Sojo, who had taken a liking to the old man, pushed him to the car amidst a flurry of fresh rose petals.

When they reached the Hall, a line of staff and estate workers were waiting to greet them with a resounding cheer.

From the reaction of the people who crowded round to shake Simon's hand, Charlotte saw that he was just as popular as his grandfather.

The reception, a miracle of organisation considering the speed it had been put together with, went extremely well, while Charlotte played the part of a happy, smiling bride.

Lunch, served by a local catering firm, proved to be excellent, and champagne flowed freely. Apart from a handful of friends who had been invited by phone, most of the guests were staff and estate workers.

Mrs Reynolds, wearing a striking black hat that made her look like a member of the royal family, was seated at the top table on Sir Nigel's left.

Sojo was sitting next to the best man, a pleasant, modest young man, with short fair hair and round amber eyes that made him look a little like an amiable teddy bear. Though Charlotte had warned her friend that his father was an archbishop, she was flirting with him shamelessly.

He appeared to be enjoying it.

By the time a few short speeches had been made, Simon seemed to have relaxed and thrown off his serious mood, but, though he was attentive to his new bride, his attitude was courteous rather than caring.

He put an arm around her while together they cut the cake, but in spite of being physically close, he still seemed distant, as if he was simply going through the motions.

When they had been discreetly warned that the car, their luggage already in the boot, was waiting to take them to the airport, Charlotte touched the Carlotta Stone and said, 'Perhaps you should put this in the safe?'

'Practical as well as beautiful,' Simon said to his grandfather, as he unfastened the jewel.

A moment or so later, with Sojo in attendance, Charlotte slipped upstairs to change into her going-away outfit.

'You still don't seem very happy,' Sojo commented shrewdly, as she helped Charlotte remove her headdress and wedding gown. 'For heaven's sake, don't let this Cinderella-Rockefeller business spoil things.'

'It's not that,' Charlotte said.

'So what is it?'

'Simon seems so strange and withdrawn, as if he's regretting marrying me,' she answered unhappily. 'You must have noticed.'

'Rubbish!'

'I hope you're not going to try and tell me he looks the epitome of a happy bridegroom?'

'No, I'm not. But men react differently to weddings,' Sojo said matter-of-factly. 'Just because he isn't bubbling over, it doesn't mean he's changed his mind. Some men take the whole thing very seriously. And perhaps he's tired—don't forget he must be under a strain, anxious about his grandfather. As soon as you get away on your honeymoon he'll be himself again, you'll see.'

Much cheered, Charlotte picked up her bouquet and went down to join Simon, who was waiting in the hall.

Together they said goodbye to Sir Nigel, who, though still smiling and in excellent spirits, was looking exhausted, his face grey and drawn with pain.

Brushing aside their concern, he said calmly, 'I intend to go straight to bed as soon as I've waved you off.'

'I'll call the nurse,' Simon offered.

'No need. Miss Macfadyen has offered to see me upstairs before she goes back to London. Now, off you go or you'll miss your plane. Safe journey.'

'I'll ring when we land at Rome,' Simon promised.

'Bless you both. This has been one of the happiest days of my life.'

As Charlotte stooped to kiss his cheek, he added, 'My dear, no grandfather could have been prouder.'

Sojo, who had been waiting in the wings, appeared at his side to take charge of the wheelchair. Then they and the rest of the guests followed the newlyweds out into the sunshine.

When they reached the car amidst a flurry of rice and rose petals, to the accompaniment of some loud cheering, Charlotte turned and threw her bouquet.

As she had hoped and intended, Sojo caught it and, grinning, blew her a kiss.

Having helped his new wife into the car, Simon climbed in beside her, and after one last wave they were off, through the archway of yew, and bowling down the drive.

With a good eighteen inches of space between them, instead of being lovers, newlyweds, husband and wife, they could have been a couple of strangers forced to share their transport.

She had hoped that once their journey was underway he would turn to her, put an arm around her, perhaps give her a kiss. But he did none of those things. Instead he sat looking straight ahead, to all intents and purposes deep in thought.

Glancing at his handsome profile, the high forehead and angular cheekbone, the sweep of thick, dark-gold lashes and the strong nose, she felt a fierce longing that was almost pain. Along with that was a growing resentment that he should treat her so cavalierly.

But perhaps that was unfair. As Sojo had suggested, he might be tired or stressed, and no doubt he was concerned about his grandfather. Maybe it was up to her to make the effort that would bring them closer.

After a moment, she ventured, 'Sir Nigel was absolutely marvellous. I don't know how he managed to find the strength.'

'Sheer will-power,' Simon answered briefly.

'I only hope he hasn't seriously overdone it.'

'I've no doubt he has, but it was his choice to keep going, and, knowing Grandfather, I'm sure no one could have persuaded him otherwise.'

He relapsed into silence, and, unwilling to risk another dismissal, she turned away and, feeling the prick of unshed tears behind her eyes, stared out of the window.

Perhaps he picked up her keen disappointment, because after a moment he began to make polite conversation, which was worse than not speaking at all. It only served to emphasise the yawning chasm that lay between them.

When they arrived at Leonardo da Vinci Airport he phoned Mrs Reynolds and was reassured to learn that his grandfather, after being given a painkilling injection, was sleeping peacefully.

Charlotte, who had been greatly worried about the old man, said a silent prayer of thanks.

A hired car was waiting for them, and, their small amount of luggage stowed in the boot, they set off for Costanzo, a small medieval town in the hills just outside Rome.

It was a lovely evening, the balmy air silky dark and scented with myrtle, the star-studded sky the colour of blueberries.

As they began to climb steadily, against the fairy-tale backdrop of the towers and turrets of Costanzo, lights twinkled and shimmered, lending the kind of enchantment that would have been lost in a city. It was cooler in the hills, and mingling with the night scents was the fragrance of woodsmoke.

Once again Charlotte felt the prick of tears behind her eyes. If she and Simon had been in tune the journey would have seemed romantic, magical. Instead it was laced with a poignant regret for what might have been.

Rather than a hotel, Simon had chosen to stay at the Villa Bernini, a small, family-run guest house. It proved to be colour-washed and picturesque, with asymmetrical windows and steeply angled gables. Its garden, complete with the ilex and cypress trees which gave that fundamentally Italian look, dropped away down the hillside in a series of terraces.

As they drew up on the lighted apron in front of the *casa*, Signora Verde appeared to greet them. Plump and smiling, she broke into a flood of liquid Italian which Simon answered fluently.

Offering him a large key, she indicated a flight of curving stone steps on the right, which led up to a low wooden door.

'Signora Verde thought it was appropriate to give us a small, self-contained apartment she calls the honeymoon suite,' he translated for Charlotte. 'Unless you would prefer to be in the main house?'

Thinking bitterly that with their present estrangement the honeymoon suite seemed anything but appropriate, she shook her head silently.

Taking the key, he thanked the smiling *signora*, who wished them *buona notte* before going back inside.

Having led the way up the steps, each of which held a stone pot filled with trailing scarlet geraniums, Simon unlocked the door, and, ducking his head beneath the low lintel, ushered Charlotte into a room that was white-walled and candlelit.

A faint night breeze made the candles flicker and set the shadows dancing, as though the room was alive and full of movement.

As he followed her in, she glanced at him, hoping against hope that in this idyllic setting he would take her in his arms and kiss her, miraculously put everything right.

But his expression and his voice no more than civil, he said, 'I'd better fetch our luggage and garage the car before we have supper.'

He went out again, closing the door behind him.

Deflated, angry with herself for being foolish enough to hope, Charlotte slipped off her jacket and looked around. The room was charming, long, and low, and simply furnished. Its windows were high, with uneven panes and wide stone sills.

Waiting for them on the wooden table was a cold meal of meat, cheese, salad and crusty bread. A large earthenware bowl was piled high with colourful fruit, and a carafe of wine glowed a deep ruby red in the candlelight.

Though it all looked delicious, she felt anything but hungry.

In the mosaic-tiled hearth a black wood-burning stove,

with a cushioned couch drawn up in front of it, glowed a welcome. It was flanked by a coffee-table on one side and a basket of gnarled apple-wood logs on the other.

To the right, a door led through to a minute kitchen with a microwave oven, a fridge, a toaster and a coffee machine.

On the opposite side there was a bedroom and a bathroom. The old-fashioned double bed was high, with a thick feather mattress, a pile of lavender-scented pillows and a sun-faded, rose-coloured eiderdown.

It was a romantic bed. The kind of bed you would find in a fairy story. *Their honeymoon bed.*

Except that after the way he'd been treating her, she couldn't believe it really *was* their honeymoon. She felt less like a bride than some cast-off, rejected without knowing why.

When they had spent the night at Owl Cottage he'd been ardent and fiery, a passionate lover who had wanted her, who had pressed her to marry him.

As soon as she had agreed, he had…no, she couldn't say *ignored* her, but he had stepped back, distanced himself.

So what had gone wrong? she wondered helplessly. Why had he persuaded her to marry him if he didn't really want her?

She couldn't believe it was simply because she might be pregnant. These days an unplanned pregnancy wouldn't even raise an eyebrow. Her mother would have been the only one to be shocked.

Nor could she credit that he had done it simply to please his grandfather.

Though she felt sure Simon would go through fire and water for the old man, when there were plenty of beautiful, aristocratic women to choose from, she couldn't see him tying himself to a little nobody he didn't want for the rest of his life.

Or perhaps he didn't intend the marriage to be permanent? Maybe, at some future date, he had divorce in mind?

Yet he had made his wedding vows as if he had every intention of keeping them.

So long as ye both shall live... Until a few days ago that thought would have pleased her; now she felt miserable and uncertain. Had marrying Simon been a dreadful mistake?

If it was, it had incurred a life sentence.

Her mother's voice seemed to echo through her head. *'Marry in haste, repent at leisure.'*

A cold chill ran through her. She didn't want to spend the rest of her life repenting, and being married to a man she loved, but who didn't love her would be soul-destroying.

But if it *had* been a mistake, it was too late.

Or was it?

Suppose their marriage wasn't consummated—and if Simon's recent behaviour was anything to go by, he wouldn't want it to be—surely it could be annulled?

Her mind a confused jumble of thoughts, Charlotte returned to the living-room.

Opposite the stove, a door made up of small uneven panes of glass gave on to a side-balcony with a stone balustrade. Opening the door, she stepped out into the cool night air.

She was standing looking over the curve of the hill to the plain below, where a few pinpoints of light pricked the darkness, when she heard Simon return and carry the luggage through to the bedroom.

A few seconds later a light footfall approached, and his lips brushed the warmth of her nape.

On a reflex action she spun round, exclaiming, 'Don't touch me!'

There was a moment's silence, then he said mildly, 'You're hardly acting like a bride.'

'You've hardly been treating me like one,' she pointed out stiffly.

'I intend to tonight.' He lifted a hand and touched her breast.

All the frustration and bewilderment of the past few days,

the growing misery and resentment, spilling over into anger, she knocked it away.

'If you think you can blow hot and cold, practically ignore me and then expect me to fall into your arms when it suits you, you're mistaken.'

Infuriatingly, he laughed. 'So my meek little wife does have some fighting spirit... Sojo seems to think you're vulnerable, defenceless, unable to stick up for yourself. If she could see you now she'd be proud of you.'

His making fun of her was the last straw.

Brushing past him, she went into the living-room and headed blindly for the outer door.

Simon reached it first and, his back to the solid wood, asked mockingly, 'You're not thinking of leaving, I hope?'

Lifting her chin, she said, 'If you imagine for one instant I'm staying here...'

'As things are, you don't have much option.'

With more boldness than she felt, she informed him, 'That's where you're wrong. Now, if you'd please get out of my way...'

'So what do you plan to do?'

'I shall ask Signora Verde for a single room inside the house,' she said coldly.

He shook his head. 'I think not. For one thing it would shatter all her romantic illusions, and for another you're my wife—'

'In name only.'

'You sound as if you intend it to stay that way.'

Recklessly, she said, 'I do.'

'I'm afraid I have other ideas.'

'That's too bad.' She made to push past him.

An instant later she was swept off her feet and into his arms.

She began to struggle fiercely. 'Put me down. I can't bear you to touch me.'

Holding her easily, he said, 'You know you don't mean that.'

His tone was patronising, as though he were speaking to a rebellious child, and, seeing red, she cried, 'I *do* mean it. I hate you!'

'You may be angry with me, but you still want me.'

'I *don't* want you.'

Crossing the room, he laid her on the couch and sat down beside her, effectively trapping her there.

Brushing a tendril of dark, curly hair away from her cheek, he said, 'My sweet little liar, you know quite well that you've wanted me from the word go.'

Heat flooded her cheeks. No wonder he was so confident. From their very first meeting he must have seen quite clearly the effect he had on her, and known she would be easy game.

She felt angry, wounded, somehow betrayed.

Fury and bitterness mingling inside her, she cried again, 'I *don't* want you. If you touch me it'll be rape.'

'An ugly word for an ugly deed. But somehow I don't think so.'

Desperately, she reiterated, 'It *will* be.'

Looking sardonically amused, he said, 'I'm quite sure I can prove otherwise, to your satisfaction and my own.'

His casual arrogance stung. 'You're a conceited swine,' she accused hoarsely.

'You wanted me at Owl Cottage.'

Hating his certainty, needing to destroy it, she gritted her teeth and proceeded to tear to shreds the web of magic that night had spun. 'That's not surprising, I was missing my current boyfriend.'

A white line appeared round his mouth, and just for an instant she thought he was furious enough to strike her. But his self-control never wavered, and she knew she'd been wrong.

'Frustration's hell,' he agreed silkily, 'and as you've been cooped up at the Hall for several nights with no company...' He let the sentence tail off.

Hoist with her own petard, she wished she'd kept her mouth shut.

As though reading her thoughts, he smiled grimly.

Her voice unsteady, she said, 'I still don't want to be forced.'

'You won't be. If I can't make you want me, let's say within five minutes, I promise I'll go and leave you in peace.'

A lot could happen in five minutes.

Afraid that, in spite of everything, he might succeed, she blustered, 'I've absolutely no intention of staying here while you—'

He bent his head and covered her mouth with his, stopping the flow of words.

Rather than an assault, his kiss was light, with no sense of urgency, as though he had all the time in the world.

She should have been on her guard, but that leisurely, unthreatening kiss lulled her into believing she could easily withstand him.

Unconsciously some of her tension relaxed.

As though in response, his tongue-tip traced the curve of her lips and slipped between them to stroke the sensitive inner skin.

He felt her shudder, and changed to a series of soft baby kisses that coaxed and invited, until without conscious volition her lips parted beneath that light, persuasive pressure.

Taking immediate advantage, he deepened the kiss, exploring her mouth with a thoroughness that made her stomach clench and her heart beat faster.

Afraid once more, she tried to turn her head away, but he took her face between his palms and tilted it to accommodate his wishes.

That gentle, but determined, mastery sent her head spinning and gave rise to a kind of drugging excitement which grew and absorbed her, weakening her desire to resist.

Lost in the sensations his mouth was creating, she didn't realise he had unfastened the buttons of her dress and slipped it off her until one hand slid her bra strap aside and cupped the soft, naked curve of her breast.

When his mouth closed over the nipple she gasped and made an attempt to push him away. But it was too late, already she was caught and held in that web of sensual delight that allowed no escape.

Easing her briefs down over her slender hips, he ran his fingers into the nest of silky dark curls, and within seconds she was overwhelmed by longing, racked by a fierce need that banished any last traces of resistance.

Close to her ear, he whispered, 'Ready to admit you want me?'

She didn't answer.

Aware only of those long, lean fingers that were relentlessly, but with maddening slowness, discovering the very core of her, she was mindless, lost to the world, her whole being intent, focused on what he was making her feel.

Drawing away, he repeated the question. 'Ready to admit you want me?'

'Yes,' she said thickly.

'I'd like you to be certain. Tomorrow morning I don't want any regrets or recriminations, any suggestion that I forced you... So if you want me to leave, I will.'

'I don't want you to leave.'

'What do you want?'

Her voice husky, she said, 'I want you to make love to me.'

'Sure?'

'Yes.'

While, with deft hands, he stripped off first her remaining clothes and then his own, she waited impatiently, lost, outmanoeuvred, forced into submission by her own weakness, ready and willing to give him whatever he might ask.

He asked for nothing. With an urgency that sent her up in flames, he just took.

But in taking, he gave in abundance. The driving force of his body making pleasure spark through her, tingling like electricity. Pleasure that climaxed in an explosion of sensation and flashing colours like a rainbow of fire.

When he lifted himself free and sat up, she lay for a little while, blind and deaf and stunned by the sheer power of it.

Yet despite all the pleasure, she felt a bleak disappointment. That had been just sex. Wonderful sex, admittedly, but no more than that.

Their coming together had made no real difference. It had altered nothing. She had wanted to feel like a wife, loved and cherished. Instead he had turned away from her without even a word or a kiss.

Tears gathered behind her eyes and threatened to fall. She covered her face with her hands.

'What's wrong?' Simon's voice asked sharply. 'Did I hurt you?'

The answer was yes, but not physically.

'No.' The denial was muffled by a sob.

Dissatisfied, he pulled her hands down and, in the flickering light from the candles, studied her face.

She looked pale and woebegone, her beautiful grey eyes brimming with tears she was struggling not to let fall.

His voice impatient, he said, 'I suggest you tell me what's wrong.'

'What could possibly be wrong?' she asked bitterly.

He looked angry. 'You're my wife. You said you wanted me to make love to you.'

'Yes, I know I did. But that wasn't love. It was just lust… You didn't treat me like a wife.'

His jaw tightening, he demanded, 'What did I treat you like?'

'Like a hooker,' she said brutally. 'Like someone expected to give value for money, but who wasn't worth any emotional commitment.'

In a single swift, angry movement he jumped to his feet and, gathering up his clothes, stalked through to the bathroom. A moment or two later she heard the shower running.

However she had envisaged her wedding night, it hadn't been like this. Without her having any idea *why*, everything had gone wrong, and from being on top of the world she had plumbed the depths.

Sitting on the edge of the couch, she folded her arms over her stomach as though to hold in the pain, while the tears spilt over, running down her cheeks in a steady, silent stream.

She felt bereft, devastated, emotionally destitute, left in the ruins of all her hopes and dreams like a survivor of some catastrophe.

So now what was she to do? How could she stay with a man who so obviously didn't care about her?

But how could she not? For whatever reason, he had married her, and, though she might regret it, she was still Simon's wife... And there was Sir Nigel to consider. For his sake she would somehow have to hide the heartbreak and make the best of things.

CHAPTER NINE

WITH a great effort of will she stopped crying and wiped her cheeks with the back of her hand. She had just pulled on her silk slip with unsteady fingers, when Simon strode in.

She noticed how relieved he looked to find she was still there, and she guessed that he had half expected her to have flown.

He was wearing a navy-blue towelling robe loosely belted around his lean waist, his feet were bare and his still-damp hair was rumpled.

Coming over, he tilted her chin. As he looked down at her ravaged face, his expression softened. 'I'm sorry,' he said abruptly. 'If you hadn't made me furious by mentioning your previous boyfriend...'

Letting the words tail off, he repeated, 'I'm sorry. I had no right to treat you that way.'

Once more the unbidden tears came.

'Don't cry... Please don't cry...' He took her in his arms and held her close, cradling her dark head against his chest. 'I'd never intended our wedding night to be like this.'

His concern was comforting. But though he was being kind to her now, he didn't really care. The reminder was like a dash of cold water.

Easing herself free, she raised her head and looked him in the face with what dignity she could muster. 'Please tell me something. Why did you ask me to marry you?'

'Why do you think?' he asked.

'That's just it,' she said helplessly, 'I don't know. I don't know why you wanted to marry me. I don't know how you feel about me...'

'Didn't we agree it was love at first sight?'

'Over the past few days you've treated me so coldly that I couldn't believe you even wanted me, let alone loved me,' she accused.

He laughed harshly. 'If you only knew what a struggle I've had to keep my hands off you. Not a minute's gone by that I haven't wanted to take you to bed and make love to you until we were both sated.'

'But if you felt like that, why didn't you—?'

'Go ahead and do it? I have certain principles, and, in the circumstances, it didn't seem right.'

So that was why he'd distanced himself. Her worst fears set to rest, she heard the angels singing.

'I've never even considered bringing a woman to Farringdon Hall before,' Simon went on. 'I've never been tempted to indulge myself under my grandfather's roof. But believe me, over the past few days I've been sorely tempted. No other woman has got under my skin the way you have, or threatened to undermine my self-control. It's almost as if I'm obsessed...'

With a sudden flash of insight, she said, 'And that made you angry?'

He answered indirectly. 'One of my best friends became obsessed with a woman. He ended up emasculated. I always swore I'd never let it happen to me.'

Nonplussed, she said, 'Oh...'

His expression relaxing, he added, 'Of course, it *might* have made a difference if he'd married her and worked it out of his system.'

Was that what *he* was doing with *her*?

As though reading her thoughts, he said, 'And before you ask, that *isn't* the reason I married you. Now, feeling better?'

She nodded.

'So how about a bite to eat? Then as it's such a lovely evening, we could take a stroll before going to bed and beginning our honeymoon proper.'

'Yes, that would be nice,' she agreed, a tingle of anticipation running through her. 'But if you don't mind, I'd like a shower first.'

'Of course I don't mind.' With a grin, he added, 'Unlike Napoleon, I do like my women clean.'

Then, with a gleam in his eye, 'In fact, as I'm not yet dressed myself, I'll be delighted to come and give you a hand.'

Her shower proved to be the longest and most erotic she had ever taken as, with effortless ease, he rekindled the desire she had thought satisfied.

By the time he licked the drops of water from her taut dusky-pink nipples and towelled her dry, she was on fire for him again.

But without making any attempt to satisfy the desire he'd aroused, as soon as she was dressed he seated her at the table and sat down opposite to watch her face in the candlelight.

When the simple, but enjoyable, meal was over, he asked, 'Ready for that stroll?'

If he'd suggested going straight to bed she would have accompanied him willingly, eagerly, but, still too shy to suggest it herself, she just nodded.

Taking both her hands, he pulled her to her feet, and, leaving the candles to gutter out, they set off at a leisurely pace, the cool, crisp, night-scented air seeming to crackle like Cellophane.

It was incredibly romantic. The indigo sky was embroidered with stars, and a glowing crescent of moon sailed high over the trees, while a few trailing wisps of pale, diaphanous cloud picked up its light and gleamed like silver veils.

As though determined to make up for the bad start, he walked with his arm around her waist. And when they stopped to look at the ruins of an old *castello* he kissed her with a sweet, seductive thoroughness that made her even more impatient to get back to the Villa Bernini.

When they had climbed the stone steps and opened the door, it was to find the remains of supper had been cleared away and both the candles and the stove replenished. A pot of coffee was standing in the hearth, and on the low table a bottle of brandy and two glasses issued a mute invitation.

Sitting on the couch together, they drank coffee and sipped the rich golden brandy before going to bed to make long, delectable love.

He knew just where to touch her to give her the most pleasure, and as well as being subtle and sensitive, he was skilled and inventive. With an instinctive knowledge of the female body and libido, he was able to satisfy, and then rekindle, her desire at will.

Before finally falling asleep in his arms, she had lived almost every sexual fantasy she had ever imagined, and some she could never have imagined in a million years.

Charlotte surfaced slowly next morning with a feeling of utter contentment. Sun slanting in through the high window lay warm on her face, and she could smell newly baked bread and coffee.

Sighing, she stretched luxuriously. She was a wife. Married to the man she loved. She wanted to shout it from the rooftops, to let the whole world share this sublime happiness.

She was still basking in the glow, when Simon appeared carrying a breakfast tray. He was dressed in smart-casual trousers and a fine black polo-necked sweater which suited his blond toughness, and made him look more macho than ever.

'Good morning,' he greeted her.

'Good morning.' She sat up, dark hair tumbling in loose curls around her shoulders, and tucked the eiderdown under her arms.

When he'd settled the tray across her knees he sat on the bed beside her, and said cheerfully, 'I've just phoned home. Grandfather had a good night and he's still sound asleep.'

'I'm so pleased,' she said sincerely.

Leaning forward, he kissed her on the lips—a sweet, lingering kiss that held the faintest hint of toothpaste and aftershave. 'I thought you would be.'

As they drank coffee and ate fresh rolls and delicious apricot jam, he queried, 'So what would you like to do today?'

Dreamily, she said, 'Whatever you'd like to do.'

'I'm pleased to see I have an accommodating wife.'

She batted her eyelids at him, Sojo-style. 'Would I be any other?'

He laughed with a flash of white teeth. 'Perish the thought. So how about some positive feedback?'

'What are the choices?'

'As I see it, there are three. We could have a leisurely drive through the surrounding countryside and lunch at some small *taverna*... Or we could go into Rome and take a look at some of the sights—that is, if you're not too tired?'

Licking jam from her fingers, she told him, 'I'd love to see Rome.' Then with a teasing glance from beneath long, thick lashes, 'That is, if *you're* not too tired?'

'Feeling sassy, eh?' Then with a hint of mock-menace, he mock-threatened, 'If you continue to sit there looking so enticing I could well decide on the third alternative...'

Realising that the eiderdown had slipped, and he was admiring her bare breasts, she hitched it up and anchored it once more beneath her arms, before asking a little unevenly, 'The third alternative?'

His brilliant green-gold eyes met and held hers. 'Spending the day in bed while I ravish you to my heart's delight, and yours.'

The erotic words made heat rise in her body.

'So which is it to be?' He took her hand and kissed it, glancing at her from beneath his lashes.

The warmth of his mouth against her palm sent a shudder through her. He was testing, or enticing, she realised. Probably both.

Trying to hide just how much he affected her, she said lightly, 'I don't think I'm strong enough to be ravished at the moment, so if it's all the same to you, I'll settle for Rome.'

He sighed. 'How to put a husband in his place. Oh, well, there's always tonight...'

The Eternal City was even more fabulous than she had imagined, and as they did what Simon described with a grin as 'a whistle-stop tour' the day passed in a kaleidoscope of colourful sights and sounds and lasting impressions.

Enjoying the warm September sunshine, they threw coins into the spectacular Trevi Fountain, strolled from the Piazza di Spagna up the flower-filled Spanish Steps to the Trinita dei Monti, and visited the Pantheon.

Then near the Campo dei Fiori, in the oldest part of the city, they stopped to eat a tasty lunch beneath a blue and white striped umbrella. They had just reached the coffee stage when, intending to ring the Hall, Simon felt in the pocket of his light jacket for his mobile and discovered it was gone.

'Stolen?' Charlotte asked in concern.

'I'm afraid so,' he said ruefully. 'As things are, it's a nuisance, to say the least. But it's my own fault. Knowing how skilled Italian pickpockets can be, I should have been a great deal more careful.'

As soon as his cup was empty, he excused himself and went into the restaurant to use the public phone.

When, after a minute or so, he returned, she asked, 'How is your grandfather?'

'Surprisingly he appears to be suffering no ill-effects. He's even managed to eat a good breakfast.'

'That's great! I take it you've spoken to him?'

'Yes, and he sounds in fine form. He asked me to give you his love.'

Her face lit up. 'How sweet of him!'

'You're fond of him, aren't you?'

'Yes.'

'I'm glad about that… More coffee?'

She shook her head.

'Then let's go. I suggest the Roman Forum next.'

Her lips smiling and her heart as light as a feather, she allowed herself to be hurried off to begin another busy round of sightseeing.

Having parked the car, they walked through the magnificent but melancholy, weed-grown ruins of the Forum, and on to the nearby Colosseum.

Outside its famous—or infamous—façade were one or two flower stalls, a row of buses from which a crowd of tourists had just descended, and several gleaming horse-drawn carriages.

Charlotte, an animal-lover, was pleased to see that the horses appeared to be well-fed and looked after.

Returning her attention to Simon, she found he was no longer by her side.

An instant later he appeared from the crowd and handed her a perfect red rose.

Filled with delight, she said huskily, 'Thank you,' and, her smile luminous, stood on tiptoe to kiss him.

An expression flitted across his face, which after a moment she identified as surprise and something else she couldn't put a name to.

'Why are you looking like that?' she asked.

'I was thinking what a strange woman you are.'

'Strange? In what way?' she wanted to know.

'A single flower got more response than an engagement ring.'

In an odd sort of way it had meant more. 'It was just so lovely and unexpected,' she told him.

He smiled. 'The same could be said for you. Now, would you like to go inside the Colosseum? Or shall we save it until our next visit?'

'Our next visit,' she said decidedly.

'So what else would you like to do, if we can fit it in?'

'I've always wanted to see the Villa Borghese,' she began hesitantly.

'Your wish is my command.'

By the time they reached the Villa Borghese, Rome's major public park, the sun had gone down, leaving a sky of pale aquamarine, faintly tinged with pink.

Apart from the roads that traversed it, at this time of day the park was quiet, and they strolled for a while without meeting a soul. Then suddenly a man appeared. Slimly built and not too tall, with black curly hair, he was walking quickly, head bent.

Charlotte froze, momentarily convinced she was about to come face to face with Rudy. But when he glanced up, though his eyes were just as dark, his features were all wrong.

As she stood transfixed, an edge to his voice, Simon asked, 'Someone you thought you knew?'

'Yes, but I was mistaken.'

When he said nothing further, pulling herself together, she walked on.

With the September dusk and the glow of the street lamps

came a brisk evening breeze that whipped up the fine particles of grit and carried the sharp, resinous scent of the billowing umbrella pines.

Seeing the faint shiver than ran through her, Simon queried, 'Had enough for the moment?'

Beginning to feel tired, and just a little cool, she nodded.

'Hungry?'

'Famished.'

'Then before we start back I'll take you to my favourite restaurant on the Via Veneto.'

After a romantic, candlelit dinner, they joined what seemed to be half the population of Rome, and strolled hand in hand along the brightly lit, cosmopolitan Via Veneto.

The earlier breeze had died away and the evening was balmy and still as they made their way back to the car to start their leisurely drive to Costanzo.

During the meal Simon had seemed particularly close and caring, and Charlotte was filled with a quiet happiness that completely wiped out any remaining doubt or uncertainty about her marriage.

The day, full of pleasure and gladness, a day to treasure and remember, was rounded off by that delightful journey in the blue of evening.

And there was still more pleasure to look forward to. She was thinking about the coming night, anticipating the joy of being held in Simon's arms, when they drew to a halt outside the Villa Bernini.

A little smile hanging on her lips, she picked up her bag and the rose he'd bought her.

As he helped her from the car, Signora Verde came hurrying out, a flood of agitated Italian pouring from her lips.

His jaw tightening, he asked a few terse questions, before hurrying Charlotte up the stone steps and into their apartment.

'What's the matter?' she demanded breathlessly, as she followed him through to their bedroom. 'Is it your grandfather?'

Tossing their cases onto the bed, Simon answered, 'I'm afraid so. Instead of waking properly from his afternoon sleep he slipped into a semi-coma. The doctor doesn't think he'll last until morning.'

Hastily collecting her belongings, she asked, 'But will there be a flight back tonight?'

'When Ann couldn't get hold of us she kept her head, thank God, and phoned Michael Forrester. He contacted Peter Raine, the pilot of the company jet—which luckily was between flights and this side of the pond—who went straight to Heathrow. By the time we get to Leonardo da Vinci, the plane should be waiting for us and ready for take-off.'

During the journey to the airport and the flight back to London, Simon was grim-faced and silent. A car was waiting at Heathrow for them, and they arrived back at Farringdon Hall in the early hours of the morning.

The housekeeper, white-faced and hollow-eyed, met them in the hall.

'How is he?' Simon asked abruptly.

'During one of his brief periods of consciousness we told him you were on your way, and he seems to be hanging on, waiting for you.'

Charlotte would have hung back and let Simon go up alone, but he took her hand and said firmly, 'He'll want you there.'

The doctor met them at the sickroom door, and, after nodding to them, went out quietly.

When they approached the bed, Sir Nigel was lying so still and quiet that for a moment Charlotte thought they were too late. Only when his grandson spoke to him did his lids flicker open.

Though the dark eyes looked glazed and sunken, he saw them both and smiled—a glad smile that illuminated his face.

'Charlotte, my dear… Simon, my boy…' It was just a hoarse whisper of sound. 'Come and sit by the bed.'

Steering Charlotte to the chair, Simon stationed himself by her side.

His voice stronger now, as if he'd rallied, the old man went on, 'I'm sorry to have interrupted your honeymoon, but I wanted to talk to Charlotte… To tell her—'

Anxious for him, she suggested, 'Can't it wait until you're feeling stronger?'

'No, my dear. I haven't got long…'

Taking his hand, she asked gently, 'What was it you wanted to tell me?'

'Perhaps you know I had two younger sisters, Mara and Maria? Mara died when she was still a child…'

Wondering if he was rambling, she said, 'Yes, I saw her portrait.'

With an unsteady hand he indicated the portrait of a young woman with dark hair and a heart-shaped face propped up on top of a bookcase. 'That's Maria… They were identical twins.'

'I can see the likeness.'

'I've kept it in my closet since it was removed from the gallery when she ran away from home after a family row…'

Hearing the dying man's laboured breathing, Simon suggested, 'Shall I fill in the details…?'

At his grandfather's nod, he began, 'Maria was just seventeen and pregnant when she ran away. Her parents were deeply shocked and washed their hands of her. The following year she wrote to Grandfather to say she'd given birth to a baby girl. There was no address on the letter. She never contacted him again, and after a couple of attempts to find her—'

'I'm ashamed to say I gave up trying...' Sir Nigel broke in huskily. 'When I realised I only had a few weeks to live, I asked Simon to try and find either her or her offspring...'

He glanced at his grandson.

'Because I was due in the States,' Simon continued, 'I hired a private detective. To cut a long story short, he discovered that Maria Bell-Farringdon had changed her name to Mary Bell, and had married a man named Paul Yancey. Which led him to you...'

Feeling completely disoriented, as though she was spinning in space, Charlotte simply stared at him.

'I used the Claude Bayeaux books as an excuse to get in touch with you...'

When she could find her voice, she said wonderingly, 'So Maria was my grandmother...'

Sir Nigel's thin fingers tightened on Charlotte's. 'Yes. You're my great-niece.'

It was an emotional moment, and, her grey eyes swimming with tears, she leaned forward to gently kiss his cheek. 'I'm so pleased you found me, so pleased we're related.'

'So am I, my dear, so am I... But there's a lot more to it than that. There's the Carlotta Stone...'

Once again his glance implored Simon to go on.

Addressing Charlotte, Simon obeyed. 'You know how the Carlotta Stone came into the family. What you don't know is that for generations it's been passed down to the eldest of the female line on her eighteenth birthday. It should have been your grandmother's, but by then she had vanished. As both she and your mother are dead, it belongs to you.'

Looking at the old man, whose eyes were fixed on her face, she said, 'So that's why you said it was mine to keep, whatever happened.'

His voice weaker now, he said, 'Yes, my dear, it's yours

by right. I hope that when you and Simon have a family, it will go to your firstborn daughter… May God bless you both. I hope you'll be as happy as you've made me.'

As though his strength was ebbing fast, he sighed and closed his eyes. After a few moments, he breathed, 'Don't either of you be sad…'

They were the last words he spoke and some half an hour later, with them still by his side, he slipped peacefully away.

Dawn was streaking the sky before they went to bed, and it was lunch time before Charlotte awoke. Just for a second or two she was disoriented, until she realised it was Simon's room, Simon's bed.

She was alone, and instinct told her he had been up for some time. She still felt tired, while sadness and a kind of wonder enveloped her like a miasma.

It seemed strange to think that she belonged to the aristocratic Farringdon family, that Sir Nigel was…had been…her great-uncle.

In the short time she had known him she had come to like and admire him, and with a raw ache of regret she found herself wishing she had had more time to spend with him, to really get to know him. Time to ask him about her grandmother.

All she knew about Maria and her twin was that they had been identical. She would have liked to know more.

Her thoughts going off at a tangent, she wondered why, when Sojo had noticed the likeness between Mara and herself, Simon had said nothing. Why hadn't he told her? Why had he rushed her into marriage without admitting they were second cousins?

She recalled how, on that first Sunday, after they had all finished discussing the wedding arrangements, Sir Nigel had taken her hand and said, 'Would you be kind enough to keep me company for a little while? I'd like to talk to you.'

With sudden clarity she knew he had been about to tell her then, and Simon had stopped him. Why?

Questions seethed in her brain. Important questions. Questions she needed answers to.

Her suitcase was standing on a low chest next to Simon's, and after finding fresh clothes she showered and dressed and hurried down the stairs to find him.

As she reached the hall, the housekeeper appeared. She too looked tired and sad.

As though reading Charlotte's thoughts, she said, 'Mr Simon's in the library. I was just about to take a tray of coffee and sandwiches in, unless you'd prefer a hot lunch.'

'No, thank you, Mrs Reynolds. Coffee and sandwiches will do fine.'

Going through to the library, she found Simon at his desk. He didn't appear to be working, and she guessed he had just been sitting in a brown study.

He glanced up and she saw his expression was cool and guarded.

Standing facing him, she accused, 'When Sojo noticed the likeness between Mara and me you didn't say anything, and you stopped your Grandfather telling me.'

He made no attempt to deny it.

'Why?'

After a momentary hesitation, he said, 'I thought if you knew too soon you might change your mind about marrying me.'

'You mean because of the Carlotta Stone?'

'It's worth enough to make you a wealthy woman in your own right,' he pointed out quietly.

Desperately hurt, she cried, 'Why should that have made any difference? Unless you thought I was only marrying you for your money.'

'No, I didn't think that. But with everything going smoothly, I didn't want to rock the boat.'

'You don't think I had a right to know that we're second cousins?'

'We're not.'

'But if Sir Nigel was my great-uncle as well as your grandfather—'

'Sir Nigel wasn't my grandfather. Though I was brought up as his grandson there was no blood tie. When my father married my mother she was a young widow and already pregnant by her first husband. You are a Farringdon and so, of course, is Lucy. But I'm not.'

Feeling as if she'd been kicked in the solar plexus, with sudden blinding clarity Charlotte saw and understood everything.

'So, as Lucy is unable to have any more children, you married me because your grandfather asked you to, to carry on the bloodline.'

'That isn't so—'

Ignoring the denial, she cried, 'Well, I've no intention of being used in that way,' and, turning on her heel, she headed for the door.

Before she reached it, Simon caught her arm and swung her round. 'Listen to me! Though he was delighted by our marriage, Grandfather didn't instigate it—'

'I don't believe you! I know how much carrying on the bloodline meant to him, and so to you.' She tried to twist away.

His fingers gripping the soft flesh of her upper arm, Simon held her there. 'As far as I was concerned, the idea of carrying on the Farringdon bloodline through my own children seemed like a precious gift... But even to give Grandfather what he most wished for, I would never have married a woman I didn't want to live with for the rest of my life.'

Green eyes met and held grey steadily.

Against all the odds she believed him, and, relief replacing despair, she whispered, 'I'm sorry,' and, leaning forward, laid her head on his chest.

He drew her close and held her, feeling her tremble against him, as he stroked her hair.

After a moment they drew apart as a discreet knock announced Mrs Reynolds with a luncheon tray.

Sir Nigel's funeral was a quiet one, as he had wished, with a mere handful of friends and the staff and estate workers present.

Sojo had announced that she would take the morning off work to come, and Simon had arranged for a car to pick her up. Though she was dressed as flamboyantly as ever, Charlotte saw there were tears in her eyes.

It was a lovely, sunny day. No one wore black. And instead of a service mourning his death, there was a brief celebration of his life, before he was interred in the family tomb.

Forced to return to town immediately after the interment, Sojo was bewailing the fact that they hadn't had a chance to talk, when the car that was taking her back drew up.

The two girls hugged each other, and Charlotte promised to ring the following day.

'Oh, before I go, there's something I *must* tell you,' Sojo said in an undertone. 'While I was waiting for the car this morning, Wudolf turned up. He was just back from the States and desperate to see you. When I told you were now Mrs Simon Farringdon, he looked as if the roof had fallen in on him. I had to go through the whole thing twice before he seemed to take it in. Finally he got the message, and was he *livid*!'

'Oh, dear... What did he say?'

'Missing out the seriously bad language, it went something like this: ''Damn and blast Farringdon... But if he thinks I'm going to let him get away with it, he's got another think coming.'' Then he said, ''I know why the swine married her, but I doubt if Charlotte does...'' And he went storming off, spitting blood.'

Sounding worried, she added, 'I got the distinct impression he was out to make trouble. Though I fail to see how—'

Seeing that some people had moved within earshot, she broke off, adding quickly, 'I'll be in touch.'

As soon as the buffet lunch was over, and the funeral guests had dispersed, Simon turned to Charlotte and, his face set and serious, said a little abruptly, 'I need to drive over to the Grange to see Lucy. Though in a way she was prepared for Grandfather dying, it's still come as a blow. And of course she's very upset because, on top of everything else, she couldn't get to the funeral.'

Charlotte's tender heart bled for the girl. 'I'm truly sorry. It must be terrible for her.'

His eyes on her concerned face, he said, 'I'd like you to come with me.'

'Of course, if you want me to.'

'I think it's high time the pair of you met,' he said.

'When do you intend to go?'

'At once, if you're ready? When I spoke briefly to Lucy first thing this morning I told her to expect us after lunch.'

'I'll just get my coat and bag.'

The Grange, which was on the outskirts of Hanwick, a picturesque little market town, stood in its own grounds. A good-sized place, built of red brick, it was square and solid and reassuring, with sturdy chimney-stacks and no-nonsense sash windows.

As they drove up, Simon remarked, 'The house used to belong to Isobel Chase, Lucy's godmother. When Isobel died she bequeathed it to Lucy, who, for some strange reason, had always liked it. From the word go her husband hated the place, and tried to persuade her to get rid of it and buy a flat in London. But though she adores him, she refused to sell. Which has proved to be a blessing. At least she had somewhere suitable to come back to.'

'Has she been home long?'

'About two months.'

'It must be extremely difficult for her when she's still bedridden.'

Simon parked the car and helped Charlotte out, before saying, 'It's where she wants to be. Lucy's always had a phobia about hospitals, and the thought of being trapped in one for months on end sent her into depression. We were afraid she would give up the fight to live, so as soon as she'd had the last operation we arranged to have a suite of rooms on the ground floor of the Grange fitted out with everything she would need, including a round-the-clock medical team. Since then she's been making excellent progress, and there's every chance that she'll walk again.'

'Yes, your grandfather told me.'

'I'm glad he lived to hear the good news. He was very fond of her.'

'He surprised me by saying he thought she and Sojo would get on well,' Charlotte said.

Simon rang the doorbell before commenting, 'Yes, I can see what he means.'

They were admitted by a neatly dressed maid, who took their coats and led them to where a pleasant, grey-haired nurse was waiting.

Beaming at them, she said, 'Mr Farringdon, how nice to see you... And Mrs Farringdon... Do come this way. Lucy's expecting you.'

CHAPTER TEN

THE room she showed them into had an adjustable bed and a large amount of gleaming medical equipment, but there any similarity to a hospital ended.

Furnished as a lounge, it was bright and cheerful with a thick-pile carpet, pictures on the walls and daffodil-yellow curtains. By the bed were two comfortable-looking chairs.

'Won't you sit down? When I make Lucy's afternoon tea, I'll bring three cups.'

She smiled reassuringly at her patient and went out, closing the door gently behind her.

Sitting a little twisted in the high bed, the young, dark-haired woman, partially supported by a padded pulley fixed to the ceiling, looked scarcely more than a girl.

Charlotte's heart went out to her.

'Hi, sis.' Simon leaned over the bed to gently kiss her pale cheek.

'Hi,' she answered, but the brown eyes, so like her grandfather's, were fixed on Charlotte, a cold hatred in them.

Appearing not to notice, he sat down beside his wife and said evenly, 'Charlotte, this is my kid sister, Lucy...'

Shaken by that look of hatred, Charlotte stammered, 'I—I'm sorry about your grandfather. Though I hadn't known him long I'd grown to like him.'

There was no response, and Simon continued, 'Lucy, this is my wife...'

Her voice shrill, Lucy demanded, 'For how long?'

'As long as we both shall live,' he said evenly.

'I wouldn't bet on it. He's back.'

Simon's well-marked brows drew together in a frown. 'I

wondered how long he'd toe the line and stay out there. Still, it's been long enough.'

'Don't think he's given up.'

In a voice like steel, Simon assured her, 'There's no need to worry; I know how to keep what's mine.'

'I only wish I did.'

All at once Lucy's brown eyes filled with tears. 'I don't know how he found out, but he was absolutely furious. He said I'd put you up to it. I thought with her safely married he'd settle for what he'd got. But when I asked him to come home so we could talk, he said he was going to leave me, that when he did come back it would just be to pack his things. He's never said that before.'

Simon's jaw tightened. 'I suggest you have them packed ready for him. Instead of letting him leave you, throw him out.'

'How can you say that when you've gone to so much trouble to—?' She stopped abruptly as Simon shot her a warning glance.

His voice even, he said, 'I've never tried to hide my belief that you'd be a great deal better off without him.'

'But he's all I've got.' The tears spilt over. 'I have to at least *try* and keep him.'

'Do you honestly think he's worth keeping?' Simon asked exasperatedly.

Feeling like an interloper, and unwilling to stay and watch the other girl's distress, Charlotte rose to her feet and made for the door.

She had taken only one step when Simon's fingers closed around her wrist. 'Don't go.'

'I'm sure neither of you want me here.'

He shook his head. 'It's something you need to stay and listen to.'

Remembering the hatred in the other girl's eyes, Charlotte

begged, 'Please, Simon… This is obviously a private matter. It has nothing to do with me, and—'

Lifting a tear-stained face, Lucy cried, 'It has *everything* to do with you, and it's only right that you should stay and see what pain you've caused.'

'I haven't the faintest idea what you're talking about,' Charlotte said blankly.

'You stole my husband, bewitched him, and even though you're married to his brother-in-law, he still wants you back.'

Wondering if all Lucy had suffered had affected her brain, Charlotte said carefully, 'You're making a terrible mistake; I've never even met your husband.'

'Don't bother lying. Before Simon sent Rudy to the States you'd been seeing him for weeks…'

So Rudy was Lucy's husband…

Just for a moment Charlotte felt as if she couldn't breathe, as if all the oxygen had been sucked out of the room.

Watching the colour drain from the other girl's face, Lucy went on, 'I can always tell when he's having an affair with another woman, but it usually means so little to him that I've learnt to ignore it, to pretend it isn't happening. Sooner or later, when he's had his fun, he ditches her without a second thought. But this time it was different. He was besotted with you from the beginning, and you led him on…'

'I had absolutely no idea he was married,' Charlotte cried desperately.

'I bet!'

'You said he'd had other affairs,' Simon observed levelly. 'Do you think he usually confessed to being a married man?'

'Most women wouldn't care,' Lucy said bleakly.

'*I* would have cared,' Charlotte insisted. 'But he never mentioned a wife. He said he had a bachelor pad in Mayfair.'

Lucy shook her head. 'He hasn't.'

'But *I* have,' Simon said, 'and I'd let him have the use of it while I was away.'

Turning to Charlotte, Lucy demanded, 'Did he ever take you there?'

'No.'

'Perhaps he was scared to in case Simon found out. No doubt when you wanted to sleep together he went back to your place or you booked a room at a hotel.'

'I've never slept with him,' Charlotte denied.

'Why not, if you were sexually attracted? And you *must* have been, otherwise you wouldn't have gone out with him.'

'I admit I was attracted. But I don't jump into bed with a man just because I'm attracted to him.'

Becoming aware that Simon's sardonic gaze was fixed on her, and suddenly remembering the night at Owl Cottage, she blushed scarlet.

Head high, she looked Lucy in the face and insisted quietly, 'I've *never* been to bed with your husband, either at a hotel or at my flat.'

'I only wish I could believe that, but unfortunately I can't. I know Rudy too well. *I'm* no use to him as I am now, and he soon gets frustrated. Knowing how he can turn on the charm, I'm quite sure he got what he wanted,' Lucy insisted.

'Not from me, he didn't. I wasn't ready to make any kind of commitment.'

'Do you mean to say you never once took him home with you?' Lucy asked in disbelief.

Reluctant to give Lucy more grounds for believing the worst, Charlotte hesitated, wondering if she should admit it.

Watching her face, Simon said quietly, 'It's no use, Charlotte. I know you did. It was the night of Anthony's party.'

Suddenly everything dropped into place. Through stiff lips, she said, '*It was you!* You were the one who stared at me.' Recalling the venom in that stare, she shivered. 'You were driving that silver car which followed us to Anthony's party and then home again.'

'Yes.' Simon sighed, 'I wanted to see for myself what was going on.'

'So you *did* take him back with you,' Lucy said accusingly.

'Just that once.'

Quietly, Simon said, 'As you didn't know he was married, no one can blame you. But I need to know the truth as well as Lucy.'

'Nothing happened,' Charlotte said desperately.

'I want to believe you, but he was with you for almost two hours and when you came to the door to see him off, you were in your dressing gown.'

'It was a housecoat.'

'I watched you throw your arms around his neck and kiss him. Then he kissed you.'

'I can't deny we kissed,' she admitted miserably. 'But that was all there was to it.'

Her mouth twisted as though she was in pain, Lucy asked, 'Then how do you account for the length of time you were up there together?'

Charlotte made an effort to explain. 'We left the party early. He asked me to go back to his…Simon's flat…but I didn't want to, so I suggested he come and have supper at my place. Sojo had said she'd like to meet him, and—'

'You mean Sojo was there?' Simon exclaimed.

'Yes, of course.'

She heard his unmistakable sigh of relief, before he urged, 'Go on.'

'Because he was angry with me, he spent most of the time talking to her, while I cooked the meal.'

'Why was he angry with you?'

'The evening had been a disaster, and earlier we'd had a

slight quarrel. I hate to quarrel, and I wanted to make it up. That's why I kissed him when he left.'

'So you're telling us he only went home with you once,' Lucy demanded, eaten up with jealousy.

'He'd taken me home on a couple of previous occasions, but that was the only time I'd invited him up… And as I keep telling you, it was all quite innocent.'

Turning to Simon, she suggested, 'You can ask Sojo if you like.'

He shook his head decidedly. 'There's absolutely no need for that.'

'Why not ask her?' Lucy said. 'Do you think she'd lie or prevaricate?'

'No, I don't. Though I've no doubt Sojo is a loyal friend, I believe she's too straightforward to do either. If I'm any judge of character, she's more likely to say, "Ok, so this is how it was, and if you can't handle the truth that's your problem".'

'Then ask her. See if their stories tally,' Lucy insisted.

'It isn't necessary,' he refused firmly. 'I believe Charlotte implicitly.'

'Lucy obviously doesn't,' Charlotte said, 'so I'd prefer it if you *did* ask Sojo.'

After directing a level glance at his wife, Simon agreed, 'If you really want me to, I'll phone her tonight.'

'Do it now,' Lucy urged. 'Ask her outright if they had an affair.'

'She'll be at work,' Charlotte said. 'There's no knowing who'll answer, and the staff aren't supposed to receive personal calls.'

Lucy's eyes flashed. 'Delaying tactics until you've had time to warn her?'

'Certainly not. It happens to be a fact.' Then to Simon, 'I could try her mobile. She's always forgetting to turn it off.'

He reached for the phone on the bedside table and passed it to her. 'Try by all means, if that's what you want.'

It was answered on the fourth ring.

'Sojo, it's me,' Charlotte said quickly. 'Can you spare a few minutes?'

'If it's important.'

'It is rather. Simon would like to ask you something, and I'd be grateful if you would tell him the exact truth.'

Charlotte passed Simon the phone.

A moment later they all heard Sojo say, 'Right, fire away.'

'I want to ask you about Rudy.'

'I thought you might. Hang on, I'd better slip out the back for a minute or so… OK… So what exactly do you want to know?' she asked.

'I'd like you to tell me what happened between him and Charlotte.'

'There's not a great deal to tell,' Sojo said.

'Did they have an affair?'

'As an affair it was a non-starter, at least on her part. But then, probably because of her upbringing, she's never been one for affairs. In fact, in the two years since I moved in, I've never known her to have what I would call a serious boyfriend.'

'How many times did Charlotte bring Rudy back to the flat?' he asked.

'Only once.'

'And you were there?'

'Yes.'

'Would you like to tell me what happened?'

'They'd been to a party and she brought him home for a meal. Because he'd embarrassed her by lying to their host they'd had a bit of a tiff, and he came back with a peevish streak a mile wide. To get his own back, he turned on the charm with me and practically ignored her. That's about it, except she was concerned about the amount of wine he'd drunk and plied him with coffee before he left.'

Brother and sister exchanged glances, as Sojo went on, 'Despite his good looks and blatant sex appeal, I thought he was a nasty piece of work, and I was pleased she'd seen him in his true colours.'

'They didn't kiss and make up?'

'I believe she tried, but he was still mad. He rang briefly next morning to say he was off to the States. As far as I was concerned, it was good riddance. I was glad Charlotte had kept him at arm's length. She's innocent and vulnerable, and altogether too nice to get mixed up with the likes of him.'

'So that's the last you saw or heard of him?'

'Unfortunately not. He waited a day or two before ringing, probably hoping to bring her to heel, and by then she was at the Hall. I told him she was away, without saying where.'

'Did Charlotte know he'd been in touch?' Simon queried.

'Yes, when she rang to say she was getting married, I mentioned it to her. I wanted to be absolutely certain you hadn't caught her on the rebound, so I asked her how she felt about him. If she'd been in love with him.'

'And what did she say?' Simon almost rapped out the question.

'That in retrospect she wasn't even sure she'd *liked* him, let alone loved him. Knowing how painfully honest she is, I knew she'd want to put him in the picture, and I asked if she intended to ring him up or write to him. She said she couldn't do either. She didn't know his home address or his phone number, or where to contact him in New York. So I told her that if he rang again I'd be pleased to inform him that she was going to marry someone far nicer. Being the kind of person she is, she said she hoped he wouldn't be hurt.'

'Did he ring again?' Simon wanted to know.

'No. But first thing this morning, just before the car picked me up, he came to the flat. I told him that Charlotte was married and who to. Or should that be to whom? Anyway, I had to tell him twice before he took it in, then boy, was he livid! I don't know if this makes any sense, but he said he knew exactly why you'd married her, and that you weren't going to get away with it. He was obviously all set to make trouble, and as you're asking all these questions I presume he must have tried.'

Then hastily, 'But tell me about it some other time. If I don't get back pronto the old dragon who runs this agency will be breathing fire.'

'Just one more thing—did you know he was married?' Simon asked.

'*Married!* The deceitful hound! He told Charlotte he had a bachelor pad... Oh, heck, I'm being paged. Must dash. Tell Charlotte I'll be in touch. Bye for now.'

With a sound like a sigh, Simon replaced the phone, and asked his sister, 'Feeling any happier about Charlotte's part in all this?'

'I'm not sure,' Lucy admitted. 'She may not want him, but if he still wants her...'

'I hardly think you can blame *her* for that.'

'No, you're right.' Then to Charlotte, who was sitting white-faced and blank-eyed, 'I'm sorry. It appears I misjudged you...'

But after passing the phone to Simon, Charlotte had ceased to listen. Instead her mind had been going over the previous conversation.

Simon had said, *'I wondered how long he'd toe the line and stay out there. Still, it's been long enough.'*

And Lucy had warned, *'Don't think he's given up.'*

Simon had assured her, *'There's no need to worry; I know how to keep what's mine.'*

Then a little later, Simon suggested, *'Instead of letting him leave you throw him out.'*

And Lucy had replied, *'How can you say that when you've gone to so much trouble to—?'* before Simon's warning glance had stopped her short.

Then there had been Sojo repeating what Rudy had said. *'I know why the swine married her, but I doubt if Charlotte does...'*

As everything fell into place, and Simon's motive for rushing her into marriage became horribly clear, the pain grew and intensified until Charlotte could scarcely breathe...

That night at Owl Cottage she had given him all the love and warmth and passion she was capable of, and he hadn't even wanted her. It had just been part of a cold-blooded plan to try and save his sister's marriage...

No, not *cold-blooded*, and he *had* wanted her.

She remembered how his heart had raced, the way his breath had hissed through his teeth, the hunger of his kisses. All the same it had been a cruel and calculated seduction...

Alarmed by the other girl's stillness and pallor, Lucy repeated the apology. 'I'm sorry... I'm sorry I misjudged you.'

Feeling like someone who was mortally wounded slowly bleeding to death, Charlotte gathered herself and focused. 'I'm only sorry any of this happened. I just wish Rudy had never come into my shop. I wish I could wipe out everything that's happened in the past few weeks.'

Once again sister and brother exchanged glances.

'Please don't blame Simon too much,' Lucy said anxiously; 'he did it for me. When I realised Rudy was serious this time and I was about to lose him, I think I went a little crazy. I begged Simon to help me. He promised to find out who the woman was and do what he could... I know you must feel hurt at the moment, but when you've had a chance to think it through—'

'Don't tell me...I'll be grateful that he decided to marry me, rather than just seduce me?' Charlotte said sarcastically.

Lucy's thin face flushed.

Instantly contrite, Charlotte said, 'I'm sorry. I just hope it hasn't all been for nothing, that Rudy stays with you, if you want him so badly.'

'I'm no longer sure I do,' Lucy said slowly. 'I always knew he had his faults and I closed my eyes to them. But now I'm starting to wonder if it's worth all the pain. Your flatmate mentioned he'd been drinking that night at your place. Rudy often drank too much. He'd been drinking heavily the night of the accident. When I said he shouldn't drive, he turned nasty and insisted. He set off as though he was at Le Mans before either of us had fastened our seat belts. We'd barely gone a hundred yards when we hit a car coming in the opposite direction, skidded off the road and rolled down an embankment. When I regained consciousness in hospital, I found that, afraid of losing his licence, Rudy had told the police that I was driving. He begged me to back him up, and I did, after he'd promised me faithfully that he'd never touch another drop of alcohol. He's caused so much trouble, so much heartache... I'm disgusted by how utterly selfish and immoral he is... And, as Grandfather often said, a leopard never changes its spots.'

Then carefully Lucy went on, 'I realise how shocked and hurt you must feel at the moment, but Simon—'

Lifting her chin, Charlotte broke in, 'Oddly enough, what hurts the most is Sir Nigel's part in all this.'

'Grandfather *had* no part in it,' Simon denied flatly. 'He knew absolutely nothing about it. Because of his failing health and his concern over Lucy, we took care to keep the whole thing from him...'

There was a knock, and the nurse came in carrying a tray.

'I thought I'd bring in the tea before Lucy got too tired. She usually has a nap about this time.'

Setting the tray down on the bedside table, she asked, 'Would you prefer milk or lemon?'

Unable to bear the thought of sitting here and politely drinking tea, Charlotte was already on her feet when Simon answered, 'Thanks, but I'm afraid we have to go.'

When he stooped to kiss Lucy's cheek, she said, 'I'm sorry, it all seems such a mess.'

'Believe me, it's nothing of the kind,' Simon assured her.

'But I've caused so much trouble.'

He shook his head. 'Once Charlotte and I have had a chance to talk I'll tell you the whole story, and then you'll see things in a different light.'

Lucy stretched out a thin hand to Charlotte. 'I hope you don't blame me too much?' Wistfully, she added, 'I'd like to think that in the future we can be friends.'

Taking the proffered hand, Charlotte said, 'I don't blame you at all,' which was the truth, 'and I'm sure we can,' which wasn't.

Simon's hand at her waist, she allowed herself to be escorted back to the hall, where the maid produced their coats and showed them out.

There was a cold, heavy feeling in the centre of her chest, her mind felt numb and her legs stiff and alien as he accompanied her back to the car.

Just as they reached it, the door of the Grange opened and the nurse called, 'Mr Farringdon, Lucy would like another word...'

Opening the car door for his wife, Simon said, 'Excuse me a moment,' and went back to see what his sister wanted.

Instead of getting into the car, Charlotte turned away. Feeling as she did, she couldn't go meekly back to Farringdon Hall. Nothing could be salvaged, no reassurance could be given that would mean anything. Her brief marriage was over.

Unable to face any more, and desperate to get away, she began to walk down the drive, walking faster and faster until suddenly her fragile control snapped and she was running, crying in great, gulping sobs.

She had almost reached the end of the quiet country lane when the car slid past her and drew to a halt. A moment later Simon was barring her way.

Taking her shoulders, he said urgently, 'Don't be foolish, Charlotte. Get in the car.'

Sobbing, 'Go away, leave me alone,' she tore herself free.

'I need to talk to you,' he insisted.

When she had controlled the sobs enough to speak, she said, 'I don't intend to go back to the Hall.'

'What do you intend to do?'

'I'm going to walk into Hanwick and get a taxi to take me back to London.'

'Chickening out?'

'Opting out,' she said thickly. 'I think I'm entitled to.'

'I've no intention of letting you run away, until we've had a chance to talk,' he declared.

'The real reason you married me was to try and save your sister's marriage; what else is there to say?'

'Quite a lot. I admit that, at first, taking you away from Rudy was my main objective—'

'You can't very well deny it!'

'I know you must be feeling hurt—'

'What about *used*? Humiliated? Angry? Betrayed?' she spat out.

'Look, we can't talk standing here. Get into the car and come back home with me.'

'No, I'm going.'

'You *can't* go.'

Somehow the anguish in his voice momentarily gave her

the upper hand. 'Why not?' she demanded coldly. 'We both know I'm probably not pregnant, and I've no intention of depriving Lucy of her husband, which is all you care about.'

'Lucy called me back to ask me to get in touch with Rudy and tell him not to bother to come home. She's finished with him,' he said.

'While I can only applaud that decision, it doesn't make any difference. I'm leaving you.'

She tried to step past him, but he caught her upper arms and stopped her.

'Not until you've listened to what I have to say. If you still want to leave me then, I won't try to stop you. Though I very much hope that I can make you change your mind.'

'Absolutely nothing you could say or do would change my mind,' she announced.

His face grim, Simon said, 'Let's see, shall we?'

Before she could make any further protest, he bundled her unceremoniously into the car and slammed the door.

The journey back was a silent one. Charlotte, her chest tight, her heart like lead, felt bone-weary and cold through and through, as though all her youth and joy of living had drained away. From time to time she shivered uncontrollably.

When they reached Farringdon Hall, still without speaking, Simon helped her out of her coat and discarded his own, before leading the way to the library, where a log fire was burning.

Knowing nothing he could say would make things better and wishing, now it was too late, that she hadn't come, she hovered like a pale ghost.

'Sit down,' he ordered abruptly. Adding in a softer tone, 'Would you like some tea?'

She shook her head mutely and went to huddle by the fire, staring blindly into the flames.

He came to stand by the hearth, and even though she

wasn't looking at him she could feel the tension in his big body as he began, 'I was still in the States when Lucy asked for my help. She was beside herself, and I flew back straight away. My detective had managed to trace you as the Farringdon descendant, and I intended to approach you as soon as I'd got to grips with Lucy's problem. It was something of a shock to discover that you and Rudy's new love were one and the same. If it hadn't been for that complication I would have told you the truth straight away.'

'The whole thing seems too much of a coincidence,' Charlotte objected.

'It was,' Simon agreed grimly. 'I realised at once that Rudy must have overheard Grandfather and I talking about finding Maria or her descendants, and about the Carlotta Stone. No doubt with an eye to the main chance, he'd done some detective work himself, and tracked you down. A beautiful woman who would shortly be rich must have been right up his street. Then, contrary to form, he fell in love with you. If he hadn't got serious, Lucy wouldn't have panicked and called me. My first thought had been to settle things financially, but I realised at once that you weren't the type that could be bought off. In any case, it was no use in trying to buy off someone who would shortly own the Carlotta Stone—'

'So you decided to lose no time in seducing me,' Charlotte bit out.

'It seemed the only way. Lucy was helpless, and she'd gone through so much.'

'I suppose the car "breaking down" was part of a carefully thought-out plan?'

'Yes,' he admitted quietly.

Remembering her feelings that night, she exclaimed painfully, 'How *could* you?'

'I had no idea then what kind of woman you were,' he defended.

'You thought I was the kind who would play games with a married man.'

'I must admit that I was prejudiced against you, until the fact that you weren't carrying or taking contraceptives made me wonder. It didn't seem to fit in with the kind of woman I still thought you were.'

From the depth of her pain, she cried, 'I can understand you trying to protect your sister, and I wouldn't blame you, if only you hadn't felt forced to marry me.'

'I *wanted* to marry you.'

'So you could kill two birds with one stone,' she accused shakily. 'Not only safeguard your sister's marriage but also ensure that the Farringdon bloodline would continue.'

'To achieve both those things I would never have married a woman I didn't want.'

Ignoring his quiet protestation, she said, 'I'm leaving.'

Simon took a deep breath. 'I won't insult your intelligence by saying that I can't live without you. But I dread the thought of having to try. Please stay.'

She shook her head. 'I'd like you to begin divorce proceedings as soon as possible.'

'Is that what you really want?' he persisted.

'Yes, it is.' She sounded determined.

'Then you must have the Carlotta Stone.'

'I don't want it. Let it stay here.' She got to her feet and was heading for the door when his voice stopped her.

'Of course, it was always on the cards that you might walk away when you finally knew everything. But I'd hoped that Grandfather was right when he said you loved me.'

She turned to face him. 'Even if he was, what good is one-sided loving?'

'But it wouldn't be one-sided.'

As she stared at him, he took both her hands. 'In spite of everything, the first time I saw you my heart stood still. I couldn't take my eyes off you. I told myself I wasn't going

to fall under your spell, that it was just sexual chemistry
But once I'd made love to you I knew that, whatever you
faults, I was hooked. You were the woman I'd been waiting
for, and I had to have you with me for the rest of my life
After all our wedding plans had been made, realising I wa
storing up problems, I began to wish I'd put all my card
on the table and given you time to think it over. But I wa
afraid that if I told you the truth at that stage you would
just walk away. So I decided to go through with it and hope
for the best. Even then it was like being at war with myself
Not only was I angry that I'd fallen in love with you agains
my will, but I was also jealous to death of Rudy, and scare
stiff you'd go back to him.'

His fingers tightened on hers. 'If I *had* told you the truth
what would you have decided?'

After a moment, she said, 'If you'd told me you love
me, and I'd believed you, I would have stayed.'

Looking deep into her eyes, he said, 'I'm telling you now
I love you more than I thought it was possible to love any
woman. I'll always love you. Please believe me.'

She saw the love there and the anxiety he couldn't hide
Softly, she said, 'I believe you,' and heard his little sigh
before his arms closed around her and drew her close.

His cheek resting against her hair, he said unsteadily, '
can't tell you what that means to me.'

'Don't try. Show me.'

He caught his breath in a laugh. 'Didn't I always say you
were a practical woman?'

Leaving her for a moment, he went to turn the big, ornate
key in the lock. Then, taking her hand, he led her to the
thick rug in front of the fire.

o   'You don't think grandfather would mind?' she asked
seriously.

'Quite the contrary,' Simon said. 'I know he would approve wholeheartedly.'

'In that case...' She stood on tiptoe to kiss him, before starting to undo his tie.

REQUEST YOUR FREE BOOKS!

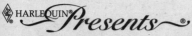

2 FREE NOVELS PLUS 2 FREE GIFTS!

PASSION GUARANTEED SEDUCTION

YES! Please send me 2 FREE Harlequin Presents® novels and my 2 FREE gifts. After receiving them, if I don't wish to receive any more books, I can return the shipping statement marked "cancel." If I don't cancel, I will receive 6 brand-new novels every month and be billed just $3.80 per book in the U.S., or $4.47 per book in Canada, plus 25¢ shipping and handling per book and applicable taxes, if any*. That's a savings of close to 15% off the cover price! I understand that accepting the 2 free books and gifts places me under no obligation to buy anything. I can always return a shipment and cancel at any time. Even if I never buy another book from Harlequin, the two free books and gifts are mine to keep forever.

106 HDN EEXK   306 HDN EEXV

Name	(PLEASE PRINT)	
Address		Apt. #
City	State/Prov.	Zip/Postal Code

Signature (if under 18, a parent or guardian must sign)

Mail to the **Harlequin Reader Service®**:
IN U.S.A.: P.O. Box 1867, Buffalo, NY 14240-1867
IN CANADA: P.O. Box 609, Fort Erie, Ontario L2A 5X3

Not valid to current Harlequin Presents subscribers.

Want to try two free books from another line?
Call 1-800-873-8635 or visit www.morefreebooks.com.

* Terms and prices subject to change without notice. NY residents add applicable sales tax. Canadian residents will be charged applicable provincial taxes and GST. This offer is limited to one order per household. All orders subject to approval. Credit or debit balances in a customer's account(s) may be offset by any other outstanding balance owed by or to the customer. Please allow 4 to 6 weeks for delivery.

Your Privacy: Harlequin is committed to protecting your privacy. Our Privacy Policy is available online at www.eHarlequin.com or upon request from the Reader Service. From time to time we make our lists of customers available to reputable firms who may have a product or service of interest to you. If you would prefer we not share your name and address, please check here. ☐

HP07